Original Edition - *Humble Beginning* -

GEN
SAN FRANCISCO

Occy Yang with Katie Gorick

GEN SAN FRANCISCO

Printed in the United States of America
ISBN: 978-0-9966935-1-6

Learn more information at:
www.gensanfran.com

ACKNOWLEDGMENTS

I wish to thank Katie Gorick, the other co-writer, for persisting through the whole process of creating this book for the last two years. Jenny Liu also has provided wonderful artworks.

This short book is dedicated to our beloved entrepreneurial generation of America that keeps our society interesting and inspiring. We also do not forget the passionate "you" who anonymously have grown a humble startup project somewhere in the world.

.

Prologue

2018.

"Welcome, viewers, to the first-ever GEN SF fashion show! I'm Leroy Bloom from Fashion Today, and we're live from the San Francisco Bay Area to bring you today's show. Now, as some of you may know, GEN SF was founded four years ago, in 2014, by ex-consultant Matthew Kim and ex-engineer Scarlet Love. If those previous careers sound strange to you, don't worry. These two are probably the last people anyone would have expected to enter the fashion industry, and yet look at the success they've had!"

The host's voice was loud over the car's speakers, and Mary Chin reached up to the ceiling to adjust the volume controls. She sat in the backseat of the driverless vehicle, which expertly navigated the narrow, winding hills of historic Boston using the latest in artificial intelligence technology. The famed and feared angel investor sat back against her leather seat and sipped at her mineral water while the announcer continued.

"There's no denying that Matthew Kim and Scarlet Love have burst onto the fashion scene in a big way these past few years. Their company is really the only one on the market today making effective and innovative use of 3D-printing technology. They've also made waves by being the first high-fashion line to exclusively use locally-sourced, eco-friendly, biodegradable materials. And they continue to push the boundaries of what's possible! As you're about to see, only one-third of the models in this show are human beings. The rest are holograms! Some of you may have seen the hologram model debuted a few weeks ago by Jinhwa Technologies, but they've certainly never been used on this scale. Perhaps because of their lack of formal fashion training, their designs simply don't look like anything else on the market today. That said, some reviewers have compared the GEN SF style to the early work of Adelina Bianchi, an Italian fashion designer from the 1920's. Oh! It looks like we're about ready to get started here, so I'll send you over to Jenny down on the runway for her commentary."

Mary Chin took another sip of mineral water and tilted her head one way, then the other to stretch out her neck. She was nearing her 50th birthday, but there was not a gray hair on her head. Her sharp, stylish bob was jet black all the way through, and there were no wrinkles to be seen around her piercing brown eyes. She was intense, intimidating, and occasionally severe, but the woman had aged exceptionally well.

Mary watched the models, both human and holographic, with a contented smile. Yes, Matthew and Scarlet had done well with this show. The designs were strikingly different than any of their competitors, pushing the edge of what was possible with modern fashion. Mary tilted her head back against the headrest and let her eyes close softly. When she spoke to herself, her voice was low and musical.

"Hard to believe it's been four years already."

Chapter 1

2013.

Fwump.

The plane touched down a bit more abruptly than necessary, and shook violently as the brake flaps engaged to slow down the aircraft. Matthew Kim rubbed at his eyes, mildly annoyed at the bumpy landing. It had been a long flight from San Francisco to New York City, and the rather large and irritable woman sitting beside him hadn't helped time pass any faster. At least he had the window seat.

He glanced down at the magazine on his lap. It was an old issue of *Fashion*, and the cover story was on the evolution of style over the last century. Matthew didn't know the first thing about fashion, but he was secretly fascinated with the ideas of style and design. His career as an investment management consultant offered few opportunities for creativity or original thought, and he envied the freedom of designers to make something new, something powerful, something timeless. He flipped to the first few pages of the cover story, to take one last look at the styles of an early 20th century designer named Adelina Bianchi, whose sharp, fearless pieces seemed to speak to some primitive desire deep within him. The large woman beside him suddenly leaned over to retrieve her bag from under the seat in front of her, catching Matthew with a wayward elbow as she did so. His reverie broken, a frustrated Matthew flipped the magazine closed and returned it to the seat back pocket in front of him.

Looking out the tiny window at La Guardia Airport, glowing against the rapidly darkening night sky, Matthew felt the uncomfortable twist in his stomach he always felt when he was stressed. He shook his head, embarrassed by his own immaturity. He was a grown man. At 32 years old, he should have outgrown his fear of his father by now. Matthew was headed to his parents' home in Fort Lee, New Jersey to celebrate Thanksgiving, but he was anything but festive. For as long as he could remember, Matthew had been a disappointment to his old man.

When the plane finally reached the gate, Matthew wasted no time gathering his things and escaping the crowded tube. He glanced at his watch. Eight o'clock. He had enough time to meet up with Jimmy and Phil and Aaron for a quick drink before he called his parents to come pick him up. He'd told them his flight got in at 10 p.m., specifically to allow himself a window to see his old college buddies. Matthew dialed Jimmy's number on his cell phone while making his way to the taxi queue just outside the airport.

Jimmy picked up after a single ring.

"Matthew! The long-lost brother has landed. How was the flight?"

Matthew couldn't help but grin at the sound of his old roommate's voice. "It was fine, if you don't like elbow room. I'm catching a taxi now. Are you guys already there?"

"Yup, you know us, no reason to delay the start of a night of drinking."

"Great. Well, I'm hopping in the cab now, so I should be there in about fifteen. I'll see you guys soon."

"Sounds good, buddy. Later!"

Matthew hung up the phone as he settled into the back seat of the taxi. The driver, a heavyset black man with a thick accent that Matthew couldn't place, turned to speak to him over the divider.

"Where to, sir?"

"Mulligan's Pub, please. It's on 2nd Avenue and –"

"I know the place," the driver interrupted curtly, turning back around and speeding out of the pick-up area.

By the time the cab screeched to a halt outside of Mulligan's, Matthew was more than a little nauseous. Still, they'd made good time, and he tipped the abrasive driver well. He took a minute to catch his breath on the curb, then entered the pub.

Mulligan's was dimly-lit and noisy with rowdy conversations and occasional cheers or jeers in response to the football game being shown on the TVs above the bar. Matthew found his friends sitting at a table in the corner, half-empty pints of beer before them. Jimmy was the first to notice him, and leapt up from his seat to offer up a hug. Jimmy was tall and lanky, with floppy brown hair. Originally from Maine, he'd moved to the city after graduating from Dartmouth. He and Matthew had been roommates their freshman year there, and Phil and Aaron had been two of their four suitemates. The other two, Eric and Cheng, now lived in Atlanta and Seattle, respectively. All six had remained close friends throughout their college years. They still kept in contact, albeit infrequently.

As Matthew took a seat and ordered a beer, Aaron clapped him on the shoulder. Aaron was short and stocky, and his face plainly showed his Mexican heritage on his mother's side. He was grinning from ear to ear.

"Hey Matthew, guess what game we're playing?"

"How should I know?"

"C'mon, just guess! You know this one."

Matthew scrunched up his face and thought hard about what they might be playing. The answer hit him with a rush of nostalgia.

"Oh god. It's not 'You Won't', is it?"

"Ding ding ding, we have a winner!"

Matthew shook his head and laughed while his old buddies exchanged high-fives. "You Won't" was a game they'd started playing back in college. Matthew had actually only played a couple times in his Dartmouth days. He'd been the least social and outgoing of his suitemates, keeping his nose in his books the majority of his days and nights. But he'd come out of his shell during business school and in his working life, and now he liked the idea of playing a drinking game with his friends.

"All right, count me in."

The rules of "You Won't" were pretty simple. They took turns challenging one another to stupid tasks, always with the taunt "you won't…" If you refused a task or failed to accomplish it, you had to finish your drink. If you achieved it, the rest of the group had to take a drink, and then you got to challenge someone else.

Jimmy leaned forward on his elbows on the sticky table. He surveyed the crowded pub for inspiration. After about a minute, he snapped his fingers.

"All right, Matthew, here it is: you won't get that blonde girl's number." He gestured toward the bar, where a pretty young woman with hair the color of butter was sipping on a mojito. Aaron and Phil exchanged fist bumps and laughed loudly. Phil shook his head.

"No chance. She's way out of his league."

Matthew raised one eyebrow, feeling uncharacteristically bold. "Watch and learn, gentlemen."

He rose and made his way over to the bar. Jimmy, Phil, and Aaron all leaned in and watched intently as their old friend elbowed his way in besides the blonde woman. They couldn't make out what was said, but the young lady was smiling and laughing at whatever Matthew was saying. He took a seat on the stool next to her, and within a minute she was scrawling something on a bar napkin. Phil shook his head incredulously.

"I can't believe this. Are we sure this is *our* Matthew Kim?"

But it didn't stop there. Matthew didn't immediately return to the table with the prized phone number. He continued to speak with the woman who was apparently NOT way out of his league, and his friends watched in amazement as he leaned over, locked eyes with her, and kissed her gently on the lips. She did not shy away, but rather reached one hand around the back of his neck to pull him closer. After a long embrace, Matthew returned to his buddies with more than a little pep in his step. He laid the napkin on the table with a flourish. Sure enough, under the name "Tiffany" was a phone number. And a winky face!

Aaron was in awe.

"Dude, Matthew, you are my hero. How did you do that?"

Matthew shrugged, a coy smile on his face. "A magician never reveals his secrets."

As he fielded high-fives and fist-bumps from his impressed friends, Matthew felt like a superhero. The next few hours passed in a blur, and not because of alcohol. He nursed the same beer all night, but he was drunk on fun. He completely lost track of time, and when he finally checked his watch, it was almost 1:30. *Shoot*, Matthew thought. He called his father, gave some weak excuse about a delayed flight, and hopped in a cab back to the airport.

Mark Kim arrived just after 2:00 a.m., visibly fuming when Matthew climbed into the car. He tapped his fingers against the steering wheel while he waited for his son to close the door behind him, then turned to face him.

"What the heck is wrong with you?"

"I'm sorry, Dad. I met up with Jimmy and the guys for a drink and just lost track of time."

"It's disrespectful to me, and to your mother. When are you going to figure out that there are other people in this world too?"

Matthew made a pathetic attempt to defend himself, but it only seemed to fuel his father's tirade. Thirty-two years of disappointment seemed to come pouring out of him over the course of the drive home. By the time they arrived back in Fort Lee, Mark stormed upstairs without so much as a "Good night" to his son, and Matthew headed straight for the minibar, no longer feeling like a superhero.

Matthew filled a tall glass with ice cold water and threw it back, closing his eyes as he let the near-freezing liquid burn his throat. After that fight with his father, he needed something to numb him against the long-buried emotions that now threatened to boil over, and ice seemed to be the right thing to counter the burning in his stomach.

He refilled the glass, sipping at the water more slowly this time. He suddenly felt dizzy, and made his way to the backyard for some fresh air. The yard was small, bounded with a neat wooden fence, and was immaculately landscaped. His mother had always loved gardening. She had an eye for color and a natural affinity for the outdoors.

As he drained the second glass, Matthew stumbled towards the center of the yard. A sparkly flash caught his eye, and he squinted toward the ground. In the middle of the lawn was a small ruby ring. For a moment Matthew stood, staring down at the ring, and then suddenly the world began to spin. Faster, faster, and then Matthew felt himself collapse to his knees as the ground and the ruby ring came rushing up to meet him. Just before he hit the ground, everything went black.

-------------------- • ---------------------

1919.

Blearily, Matthew blinked open his eyes, tasting dirt. As his fuzzy vision slowly refocused, he began to recognize the familiar shape of blades of grass in front of his face. Wide, mottled green strips shivering and swaying in the breath of a

11

light breeze. He first became aware of a dull, pounding ache in his temples, and then other sensations. The hard-packed earth beneath his face, limbs and torso. The uncomfortable poke of a gnarled tree root below his left hip. The scent of dew and moist earth under his nose, and the slight dampness of his clothing against his skin. A few warm afternoon sunbeams filtered gently through the trees around him, dappling the cool grass and decaying leaves with soft light. Matthew let his eyes drift shut again, trying to concentrate in spite of the headache. *I fell down,* he eventually remembered. *I went into my parents' backyard and I fell down. I wonder how long I've been out here?*

Taking a deep breath of crisp autumn air, Matthew spat a few times to remove most of the dirt from his mouth and then gingerly eased himself off of the ground. His head spun as he moved, and for a moment he rested on all fours, staring at the ground, waiting for the world to steady once more. Finally he pushed himself back to a kneeling position and looked around at his surroundings for the first time. And instantly he froze.

Matthew was definitely not in his parents' backyard. *Where the heck am I??* Alarmed, he snapped his head from left to right, desperately trying to get his bearings. In doing so, he sent fresh waves of sharp pain through his temples, and he gritted his teeth against the throbbing. Large trees encompassed the small grassy clearing where he'd been sprawled. *Some sort of forest?* Past these trees he could see other open expanses, as well as hulking rock formations and rolling hills. Carefully, he got to his feet.

Birds chirped in a frenzied symphony as Matthew shuffled sluggishly through the trees towards a nearby hill. He hoped the higher vantage point would provide him with more clues as to his whereabouts. As he trudged through the twigs and fallen leaves and into the clear sunlight, he replayed the previous evening in his mind. *I flew to La Guardia. I met up with Jimmy and the rest of the gang. I kissed that girl... what was her name? Tiffany? Dad picked me up. He was angry. I had a few drinks when we got back and I went outside for some air. I fell down... but where am I now?* He could not remember anything after collapsing in the backyard of his parents' house. *How did I get here?*

Cresting the top of the knoll, Matthew gasped. Even though he was not a New Yorker, he had visited the city enough times to immediately recognize the familiar sites of lightly forested land, scarred by thin, winding paths, set beneath a wide skyline of towering gray buildings. He was in Central Park.

Chapter 2

A long minute passed as Matthew stood looking around with dumbfounded wonder, his arms hanging slackly by his sides. *Did I walk here last night? Did someone carry me here? Was I drugged? Mugged maybe?* He reached for his pants pocket and found both his wallet and phone. The cash and credit cards were just as he remembered, and the phone appeared untouched, although it would not turn on. *The battery probably died since I didn't plug it in last night.* Frowning, Matthew patted down his body for bruises or other injuries that would indicate some sort of violence. Nothing. He sighed deeply. Realizing he was not going to find any answers standing around in the park, he made his way back down the hill.

With the slowly setting sun behind him, he knew he was moving east. His head was starting to clear at last, and he began to formulate a plan. Eventually he would emerge from the park onto 5th Avenue, which bordered the east edge of Central Park. From there he could hail a cab back to his parents' home. Perhaps they could shed some light on the mysteries of the previous night. Imagining his father's frustration and disappointment with this latest drunken mistake, Matthew sighed. The purpose of this visit to his parents' home had been to try to repair and restore the father-son relationship that had been slowly deteriorating over the past decade, and so far all he'd done was make things worse than ever. Guilt churned in his stomach, mingling unpleasantly with the nausea that had been gradually bubbling up to the back of his throat. *I should never drink. I have no tolerance at all.*

A blurry memory rose to the forefront of his mind. A memory of the last time he'd drank too much, about five years prior...

> *It had been December of 2007. Matthew was finally starting to settle in to his financial consulting job at SB FINANCE, and had just moved into his new condo in Redwood City. It was a Saturday, and he had spent the day unpacking the last of his small collection of boxes, furnishing the home sparsely with all his worldly possessions. Sometime in the late afternoon, he carried the final stack of broken-down cardboard boxes out to the street, shivering in the chilly breeze. As he strolled back into his warm, welcoming new abode, he sighed contentedly. He was in complete control of his life. He was independent. He was comfortable.*

15

He was a bit hungry, so he made himself a ham and cheese sandwich. As he was returning the sandwich supplies to the refrigerator, his eyes landed on the six-pack of Budweiser on the shelf. He had earned the reward, so he popped a can free. He carried his supper to the simple but sturdy kitchen table, a smooth round chestnut surface just large enough to comfortably accommodate the two matching white-cushioned chairs. Matthew leaned back in his seat and cracked open the beer. As he took the first refreshingly cold sip, he let his eyes drift shut with a smile. The office Christmas party was that evening. He'd bought himself a new tie for the occasion, as an early Christmas gift to himself. It was sky blue with thin alternating silver and black stripes, made of silk. He hoped Jennifer would notice. Jennifer was a pretty young consultant who had started working for SB Finance at the same time as Matthew. She had a quirky sense of humor and a warm smile, and he'd developed quite the crush over their first few months together.

He still had an hour to kill before the party, so he decided on a whim to call his father. They hadn't spoken in months, and Matthew was suddenly eager to share his recent successes with the man whose

approval had always eluded him. He took another long
swig from his beer, then dialed his parents' home
phone number on his cell. His mother, Seraphina,
picked up after two rings.

 "Hello?"

 "Hi Mom. It's Matthew."

 "Matthew! How good to hear from you! How
are you doing? How is work?"

 He chuckled at his mother's excited response.

 "I'm doing well, Mom. And work is really
good. Just moved everything into the new
house, too."

 "I want to see pictures of the house!"

 "Haha, I'll email you some tomorrow then.
How are you and Dad? Is he around?"

 There was a pause, just long enough to catch
Matthew's attention. When his mother spoke, her voice
carried a hint of hesitation.

 "We're just fine… Both in good health. And we
just put up new curtains in the living room.
Green ones."

 "I bet they go well with the couch in there. So,
do you think I could speak with Dad?"

 Another pause.

"Matthew, he's in one of his moods. The firm lost a big case yesterday. I'm not sure if it's a good time."

Mark Kim was a partner in a small but respected New York City-based law firm specializing in estate law. When one of New York's rich and powerful died, their loved ones often turned to the offices of Bradley, Kim, and Weston for help in protecting their inheritance. Mark and his colleagues had an excellent success rate, and he did not take kindly to losing.

In hindsight, Matthew should have listened to his mother's advice. But in that moment he was feeling good about himself, about his accomplishments, and he thought he could handle his father's bad mood and perhaps even turn it around.

"It's alright Mom. I just want to chat. Could you put him on please?"

"Okay... I love you Matthew. Thanks for calling. Here's your father."

A brief rustle, and then his father's low, clipped voice.

"Good evening Matthew."

"Hi Dad. Just finished unpacking in the new house today!"

"How is work?"

"Really good! It's a great group of people. I'm actually going to a get-together later ton-"

"How are your numbers?"

Matthew scowled. He should've seen this coming. Conversations with his dad always came back to quantifiable performance. Never mind that he was feeling happier and more independent than he had in years, or that he was making good friends at work and had his eye on the cute girl from across the office. No, Mark Kim was only concerned with what he could measure, with what he could use to definitively gauge his son's success. And in the field of consulting, that meant Matthew's stock performance.

"Seriously, Dad? Umm.... Last year was 24%. Not bad for someone of my experience."

"Hmm. I believe your cousin Andrew in Boston is averaging around 32%. Maybe you should speak with him."

"Dad, I don't need any coaching. We've been over this. I'm just... unproven. I don't have a

track record established enough to attract
many investments. I just need time, that's all."
"Matthew, all I'm saying is that you aren't
getting any younger. If you want to be
successful in life you really need to start
applying yourself. You need to develop a strong
reputation before you've been in the industry
too long."
"Really? We're going to have this fight
again?"
"There's nothing to fight over, Matthew. I'm
just telling you what it takes to have success in
business in this country."

Fuming, Matthew had thrown back the rest of
his beer and launched into a defensive tirade. It turned
out to be one of the worst fights he and his father had
ever had. When he finally slammed down the telephone
in the middle of one of his father's condescending
comments, he was already late for the office Christmas
party. Grumbling to himself, he shoved himself away
from the kitchen table and stormed to his bedroom. He
yanked off the grungy T-shirt and shorts he'd been
wearing to unpack, and threw on the slacks and dress
shirt he'd laid out earlier that day. In his rush to leave,

though, he forgot all about his new tie, still lying in the department store bag on the floor of his closet. Snagging another beer from the fridge on his way out the door, he hurried to his car and drove to the office, seething all the while.

By the time he arrived at SB FINANCE, the parking lot was nearly full. Before joining his colleagues at the party, he stopped by his small office, opened the beer can, and drank it quickly. He threw away the empty beer can in the black metal trashcan, took a deep breath, and headed to the big conference room where the holiday party was held. He stopped just in front of the tall glass doors, combing through his short black hair with his fingers and taking a breath to settle his emotions. Rolling his sleeve cuffs up twice, he straightened his shoulders and strolled into the party scene.

The party was already in full swing. Green and red decorations hung from the cubicle dividers, souped-up Christmas carols blared from speakers in the corner of the office, tables filled with snacks and punch bowls lined the walls, and the break room had been converted to a makeshift bar. Overwhelmed, Matthew forced a smile as he greeted his coworkers and began to navigate the room. Although his head was already spinning a bit, he made his way over to the break room and poured himself a glass of eggnog.

He returned to the party and made casual small talk with Jason from Human Resources. He was bored and distracted and struggled to stay focused on the conversation. Jason was babbling about his picks for the Superbowl and why some quarterback was so overrated. Matthew didn't follow football. He was of the opinion that it was a barbaric game with a needlessly complicated set of rules, but he didn't share that information with Jason.

Suddenly, across the room, Matthew spotted a tall brunette in a sleek forest green dress. It was Jennifer.

"... and there's no reason why Cutler should've been picked over –"

"Hey Jason, could we continue this conversation a little later? I just remembered I was supposed to give Jennifer the phone number of my contact at that bank on Anderson Street."

Jason stopped mid-sentence, then slowly smiled.

"Ah, Matt. Always working, aren't you? Don't forget to have fun every once in a while, buddy!"

Matthew turned away from Jason just in time to avoid being caught rolling his eyes, then made his way through the crowd to the other side of the office. Jennifer was standing in a small circle with four other young women, all of whom seemed to be laughing at some joke. Matthew kept his head down and lingered by a nearby snack table, pretending to peruse the selection of chips, cookies, and veggies and dip. After a few minutes the circle dissolved, and he seized the opportunity to intercept Jennifer before she wound up in another gathering. He took a few steps away from the snacks and bumped his shoulder against hers as he was walking by, then acted surprised to see her.

"Oh, hi Jennifer! I didn't see you there!"

"Matthew! How are you doing?"

She smiled warmly at him. Her white teeth and sparkling eyes were dazzling, and Matthew found himself temporarily distracted.

"Yes... I mean, I'm doing well! How are you?"

"I can't complain! I always love the holiday season."

23

"Oh, me too. All the decorations, the parties, the television specials…"

He trailed off, distracted by a glimmer of light reflecting off her deep brown, wavy hair. She was nearly as tall as he was, and had chosen to wear flats instead of heels. Her eyes were locked on his, and she nodded enthusiastically to what he was saying.

"Exactly! Although I think my absolute favorite part is seeing the family. I'm originally from Wisconsin, so I don't get to meet up with them very often anymore."

"Oh, where in Wisconsin?" Matthew asked eagerly, despite the fact that he knew nothing about the geography of the state.

Jennifer's emerald green eyes lit up at his interest, and Matthew melted a little inside.

"A town called Fitchburg! It's just south of Madison. I went to Wisco, so I've been close to home my entire life until I moved out here a few years ago!"

"Oh, then I bet you're definitely missing the family." He cringed inwardly at the thought of his own recent interaction with his father.

"Absolutely. I can't wait to see them all... Luckily my boyfriend and I are flying out tomorrow afternoon, so I don't have to wait long!"

The word "boyfriend" hit Matthew like a ton of bricks. Of course she had a boyfriend. She was beautiful and intelligent and fun. The three drinks seemed to hit him all at once and suddenly the world was spinning.

"Your boyfriend. Right. That sounds nice. Hey, I have to go talk to Jason about something but it was good catching up."

Jennifer looked a bit surprised but handled it well like a pro.

"Oh, of course! Enjoy your holiday, Matthew!"

Matthew stumbled back over to break room. As Jennifer's face swirled around in his mind and his father's voice echoed in his head, he poured himself another drink.

That was the last he remembered of the evening. He awoke the next morning lying face-down on his couch, still fully dressed, shoes and all. He was later informed that two of his coworkers on their way out of the party had found him sitting on the curb in the parking lot, clearly inebriated, and had called a cab to take him home. Embarrassed and ashamed, Matthew thanked his lucky stars that his father didn't know.

Matthew shook his head to clear out the unpleasant memory. It didn't do any good to dwell on the past. Besides, he was nearing the edge of the park, and could see the tops of buildings peering over the tall trees. He picked up the pace, eager to find a taxi and get home and sort out what had happened that had caused him to sleep in Central Park. Through a break in the trees, he caught a glimpse of asphalt, and he hurried forward. At long last, he emerged from the park.

Chapter 3

"Hey, look out, Mister!"

Matthew turned just in time to leap out of the way of a rapidly-moving black vehicle. Spinning around to look at his would-be killer, he realized the bizarre automobile was a Ford Model T, like he'd learned about in history class back in grade school. He stood gaping at the receding car for a few moments before he again heard the small voice.

"Are you okay, Mister?"

Matthew noticed the boy across the street for the first time. He was perhaps 12 years old, skinny, with a mop of tangled brown hair visible beneath a saggy gray cap. His worn gray breeches were a little too big for him, and his dirty red wool sweater was fraying at the seams. The boy carried a canvas messenger bag over one shoulder, which reached almost to the ground. He was looking curiously at Matthew, who had yet to respond.

"Mister?"

"Huh? Oh, yes, I'm fine, I'm fine. I never saw that car coming!"

"Gotta be careful crossing these streets! Are you from China?"

"I'm originally from New Jersey, but now I live in California. Do you live in the city?"

"Yes sir, with my Ma and my little brother Johnny. My name's Phillip." The boy walked quickly across the street and extended his hand to Matthew.

Marveling at the child's self-assuredness, Matthew shook the small hand, which had a surprisingly strong grip.

"I'm Matthew. Do you happen to know where the nearest bus stop is? I'm trying to get back to Jersey before the rush hour traffic hits."

Phillip squinted and tilted his head to one side.

"I'm not sure I know what you mean, Mister."

"Actually, I should just call a cab for a ride back to Jersey. Although my iPhone is dead… any chance you have a cell phone I could borrow?" Sure, the kid was a bit young, but lots of parents were getting their children started on technology young these days.

The boy appeared confused, and began to back away warily.

"What's the matter?" Matthew asked, concerned. "It's okay if you don't have a cell - I'll find one to borrow!"

Phillip continued to retreat, more quickly now.

"Sorry, Mister, Ma says not to talk to nutters." With that, he turned around and began to run. As he did, the oversized canvas bag jumbled against his rapidly pumping legs, and a newspaper fell to the pavement.

Baffled by the boy's behavior, Matthew strode forward and picked up the paper. He looked down at the front cover and could not believe what he saw. He rubbed his eyes and looked again. It was the New York Times. And the date was November 8th, 1919.

--------------------- • ---------------------

What kind of elaborate joke is this? Matthew thought to himself. *Who's messing with me? And where did they find a newspaper from 1919?*

When he finally tore his eyes away from the surprisingly authentic-looking newspaper, he took in his surroundings in detail for the first time since leaving the park. The towering buildings left no doubt that he was indeed in New York City. However, the skyline was different than the Manhattan he remembered. There was no Empire State Building, no Chrysler Building, no Carnegie Hall Tower. Matthew felt the world spinning around him and took a few deep, shaky breaths to steady himself. He scanned the streets for answers.

To his right, about two hundred yards in the distance, he spotted a couple strolling in away from him, heading south. He knew that Times Square and the Theater District lay in that direction. Maybe these people could provide some clues to his situation, and if not, surely the busy hub of Times Square would prove useful. He began to jog after them.

As he neared the couple, he noticed that they were quite oddly dressed. The woman was wearing a long, off-white dress beneath a thick, deep brown fur coat. Atop her raven-haired head was a wide-brimmed brown hat with an iridescent green feather protruding from it. The man was decked out in an expensive-looking light gray three-piece suit. The trousers were pleated and cuffed at the bottom, and he wore a matching gray Homburg hat. They spoke in soft, polite voices as they ambled along the road.

Matthew slowed to a walk as he caught up. He suddenly found himself feeling oddly self-conscious, and he did his best to smooth out the wrinkles in his pale blue button-down shirt before tentatively clearing his throat and speaking up.

"Excuse me?"

The couple broke off mid-conversation, stopped walking, and turned to look at him. Their faces were expressionless as they silently scanned him up and down.

"I was wondering if either of you could lend me a cell phone for two minutes? I just need to call a cab…"

The woman slowly turned to face her partner, who was squinting curiously at Matthew. After a long moment, the man took a small step towards him.

"My apologies chap, but I'm afraid I don't understand your meaning."

Now it was Matthew's turn to fall silent. He carefully scrutinized the faces of the couple, trying to detect any hint of sarcasm or humor that would indicate they were just part of some elaborate prank. Finding none, he forced himself to ask the question even though he knew it was crazy:

"What is today's date?"

"The 8th of November, if I'm not mistaken."

"And the year?"

The man's bushy black eyebrows furrowed at Matthew.

"Why, the year is 1919, chap."

Matthew closed his eyes and rubbed his temples. He stood like that for a long while, just processing. When he opened his eyes again, the couple had resumed walking, a bit more quickly than before, with the woman glancing occasionally over her shoulder back at him. They soon turned onto a side road and slipped out of view.

It's not possible, he thought to himself. *This doesn't make sense. You don't just wake up one day in a different decade... right? How could I have gone back in time?* He felt completely and utterly lost. Two more Model T's rattled past. The sun was now starting to dip below the city skyline, and Matthew felt his stomach rumble. *Maybe I'll be able to think more clearly after I find something to eat.* Jamming his hands into the pockets of his jeans, he began to move south on Fifth Avenue towards Times Square.

As he drew closer to Manhattan's thriving hub, he passed by more and more New Yorkers, some of whom stared at his clothing and gave him peculiar looks. He kept his head down, not interested in repeating his previous two interactions with strangers, both of which had ended with his new acquaintances fleeing. Moving in a fog, he didn't take any notice of his surroundings until he nearly collided with a yellow car while crossing the street.

He saw the flash of yellow and quickly extended his hands as if he could stop the vehicle with just his own strength. Thankfully, the car slammed to a stop inches from Matthew, with the tires squealing loudly. The driver leaned out of the window.

"Hey, watch it!"

Ignoring the reprimand, Matthew looked carefully at the yellow automobile. To his surprise, it was a taxi cab – a very old-fashioned taxi cab, with a black-and-white checkered stripe along either side. Eagerly, he looked up at the driver.

"This is a taxi, right? You can take me somewhere?"

Rolling his eyes, the driver scoffed.

"What are you, blind? Of course it's a taxi. You getting in or what?"

Matthew hurried around the car and hopped into the back seat.

"All right, where are ya headed?"

His first instinct was to say New Jersey, but suddenly a disturbing thought struck him. As hard as it was to believe, the world around him definitely seemed to indicate that he was now living in the year 1919. There did not appear to be anyone else from the twenty-first century anywhere in sight. That meant that no one would understand his ridiculous story of time travel. It meant that he was completely alone. It also meant that he would not find what he was looking for in Cherry Hill, New Jersey. Because in the year 1919, Matthew's parents had not been born. They did not yet exist.

Chapter 4

"Hey, you deaf, Mister? I said, where ya headed?"

Matthew snapped back to attention. He had no idea what to do, or where to go. He opened his mouth to speak, then closed it again wordlessly. He wracked his brain for ideas. Feeling the cabbie's impatience mounting by the second, finally he tried again to speak, this time with more success.

"I, uh... I guess... is there a place around here to get a bite to eat?" Then, realizing this was a dumb question to ask in a huge city, he clarified, "That you might recommend?"

The driver sighed, and turned to face his unusually nervous customer. He was a large man, with a reddish hue to his skin and broad, thick chest. His appearance was made all the more impressive by the large, well-worn black coat he wore. A dirty brown cap covered his head, although small tufts of grayish-black hair stuck out in places. A burnt-down cigarette hung from his yellow-stained teeth, and bushy gray eyebrows covered most of his heavy, protruding brow. Beneath were small, dark eyes, which now squinted at Matthew. After a long moment of consideration, the oversized man appeared to conclude that Matthew was not a threat. At worst, he was just a lost crazy person.

"Well, I suppose that depends what you like to eat," he remarked gruffly. "Say, you got money, Mister?"

"Yes, of course!" Matthew replied eagerly. He quickly reached into his pockets to find his wallet, pulling it out with a flourish. He pulled out two twenty-dollar bills and held them up for the driver to see. "See? I can pay!"

A massive hand reached back to snatch one of the bills. The thick gray eyebrows furrowed together as the cabbie squinted first at the money, then at Matthew once more.

"This some kind of joke, Mister?" he growled.

"What? No... I was just showing you that I have cash! That I can pay for a ride somewhere, that's all I was –"

"You think I'm stupid or something? That money's fake, sure as I'm sittin' here. Can't pay for my services with that, Mister."

"It's not fake, I promise!! It's just a little newer than what you're used to seeing, I swear, it's not counterfeit!"

But the huge man was not hearing Matthew's protests. He shut his beady eyes and shook his head slowly. "Can't do it, Mister. That money's no good here. Can't help ya."

Defeated, Matthew slumped back in his seat. For a long moment there was no sound in the cab but the engine idling and the muffled noises of the surrounding city. Eventually, the weary time-traveler sat upright, smoothed out his wrinkled shirt, and cleared his throat.

"Well. Thanks anyway for your time." Without waiting for a response, he climbed out of the taxi.

The darkness had deepened considerably since he'd entered the cab. Men and women hustled by in all directions, turning up their coat collars against the evening chill. A few cast sideways glances at the oddly-dressed Asian man standing in the center of the sidewalk, but most shuffled along without a second look.

Matthew rubbed his hands together to warm them up, looking around for inspiration. He began to walk back the way he came, unsure of what exactly he was looking for. After a few blocks, the faint sounds of up-tempo music drew his attention to a dilapidated storefront. Warm yellow light spilled out around the doorframe, and even in the darkness Matthew could make out the words "Willie's Tavern" painted above the door. He knew he wouldn't be able to get anything to eat, what with his money appearing counterfeit to the residents of this decade. He shivered violently as a gust of wind howled down the city street. *Maybe I can at least go inside and warm up a bit.* He hesitated, then stepped forward to enter.

Crossing the threshold to the tavern, Matthew immediately found himself caught up in a swirling sea of noise and confusion. Somewhere out of sight, reedy saxophones blasted jazz into the crowded room, and boisterous, drunken individuals danced freely through the cigarette-smoke-clouded air. Matthew collided with a number of them as he tried desperately to make it to the edge of the room, where he collapsed into the nearest booth. In the haze, it took him a moment to notice the elderly man sitting across from him. A long white beard trailed wispily from his face, and as he peered over badly-bent spectacles at Matthew, his cracked lips broke slowly into a mocking, toothless smile.

"Oh – I'm sorry, sir, I didn't mean to intrude, I was just trying to get out of the way, it's really crowded in here, and – "

"Too many of you damn chinks in here, I say!" the old man slurred lazily. With a hiccup, he reached for the half-full mug on the table in front of him.

"Actually sir, I'm from Korea."

"You're a chink, son. Damn chinks just comin' in here and takin' our jobs and dancin' with our women. Think you're better than us…" he trailed off as he looked towards the dance floor.

Matthew glanced around, unsure of how to respond. As his eyes adjusted to the lighting, he realized that while all of the women in the tavern were white, there was a mixture of white and Asian men. The Asian men indeed all seemed to be Chinese. *How very interesting*, he thought to himself. He turned back to the old man.

"And who is us, exactly?"

The old man blinked at his uninvited company.

"Whaa's that now?"

"I said, who is us? You said 'you chinks think you're better than us.'"

"Why, the proud and hon'rable men of Ireland, o' course!"

Matthew was suddenly reminded of history lessons from his youth, detailing American society in an era long ago. An era he now inhabited. He vaguely recalled one of his teachers explaining that some immigrant groups faced heavy discrimination upon reaching the United States. Among the most harshly-treated were the Irish and the Chinese. A textbook photo of a wooden sign reading "Irish Need Not Apply" floated to the forefront of his memory, as did the term "Chinese Exclusion Act". Blinking as he tried to reconcile long-forgotten chalkboard lectures and the in-the-flesh history lesson before him, Matthew realized he had inadvertently stumbled into the bar perhaps best suited for his current state; a bar inhabited exclusively by misfits and underdogs.

Perhaps it was the stirrings of some kind of latent patriotism, or perhaps it was simply that he was tired and hungry and had had an astoundingly bizarre day, but Matthew felt a strange wave of emotion wash over him as he looked around the tavern. This was a simpler time, a more honest time, a time where someone could start again. He was surprised to find that he had the impulse to stand up and join in the dancing. But before he could act on the spontaneous thought, a soft *thwunk* brought him back down to earth. He turned to see that the old man had passed out, and was now slumped face-down on the table. The sight reminded Matthew of just how exhausted he was, too.

Pushing himself out of the narrow booth, Matthew stretched his arms and legs and took a deep breath of the warm, smoky air. The old man's coat hung on a brass hook outside the booth. For reasons he didn't quite understand, Matthew picked up the coat and hung it over the snoring Irishman's shoulders. He then picked his way once more through the crowded space, and finally emerged into the crisp, dark city streets.

Now what? He was just as homeless, broke, and hungry as he'd been before he entered the tavern, but something had changed within Matthew. For perhaps the first time in his life, he was not afraid of the unknown. For the first time, he looked forward to the adventures and challenges of another day. With a small smile, he warmed his hands in his pockets and strolled back towards Central Park.

As he walked, Matthew let his mind wander. He thought about the old man, and wondered what jobs he was lamenting losing to the Chinese. He wondered, if he were to have been born into this age, what his occupation might have been. What his father's occupation might have been. Where he would have lived. What his schooling would have been like. What would New York City be like during the Great Depression? Or Prohibition? Or World War 1? He lost himself in a fantasy composed partially of primary school teachings and partially of blind imagination.

Flickering gas lights lit the city streets, casting long, wavering shadows behind Matthew as he walked. The crowds had thinned out considerably, although a few drunkards still stumbled about. When he reached Central Park, he peered into the deep blackness between the trees with only the slightest twinge of apprehension. After a brief hesitation, he stepped into the darkness. It took a good deal of straining to make out the trees and rocks by the little moonlight that made it through the treetops, but eventually Matthew found a flat, grassy clearing. With a groan, he settled himself heavily against the trunk of a large oak tree on the edge of the clearing. Crossing his arms tightly across his chest for warmth, he let his eyes drift shut, and quickly fell asleep.

Chapter 5

A soft, tropical breeze. A white sandy shore as smooth as silk. Brilliant, cerulean blue waves lapping gently, rhythmically. The caw-caw and flutter of wings of a seagull circling nearby. Warm sun caressing his skin as he reclines in a comfortable lounge chair. The cool condensation on the glass of a refreshing frozen drink. Matthew had had this dream many times before, ever since looking through a brochure for Jamaica at a travel agency near his house while under the delusion that he'd take a luxurious vacation in the near future. He'd dreamt of this place so many times, in fact, that even in his semiconscious state he knew it was a dream, and that soon he'd be cast back out into cold, dreary reality.

Unfortunately, that return to reality came even sooner than expected, as the snoozing Matthew's reclining body slipped off the tree trunk. His head and torso fell to the dewy grass with a *thwump*, and he woke with a start. He was dismayed to realize his shirt and jeans were soaked through from the damp grass, and he got to his feet to brush off the twigs and dirt from his backside. He yawned deeply and stretched his arms out over his head, savoring the gradual release of tension from his back and shoulders.

Exiting the park took much less time this time around, since he remembered the path he'd taken the previous evening to his makeshift bed. Stepping back onto the sidewalk, he continued confidently back toward the bustling center of the city. His stomach growled loudly as he walked, reminding him of the fact that he was starving. Fingering the useless bills in his pants pocket, he frowned and tried to come up with a plan to get something to eat that didn't cost money. He wondered if there was a soup kitchen nearby. *Did soup kitchens exist in 1919?* For a moment the idea of stealing food crossed his mind, but he shook his head to clear the thought. He wasn't that desperate. Not yet.

Still, he was having a hard time concentrating on anything other than finding his next meal. The sweet and savory aromas of a small corner bakery stopped him dead in his tracks. He stared ravenously through the store window at the displays full of freshly baked bread, muffins, rolls, and pastries. Inside, a line had formed of men picking up a bite to eat on their way to work and women shopping for groceries for the day. Matthew had to catch himself to keep from drooling.

A metallic *clang* broke his reverie. He looked up to see a young man dumping a tray of burnt bread loaves into the trash can in the alley alongside the bakery. The man returned the lid to the can and strolled back into the store.

That doesn't count as stealing, right? Matthew didn't particularly like the idea of scrounging through the trash, but it certainly seemed like a favorable alternative to hunting rats in the streets or taking a beating from a 1919 policeman for theft. Glancing around to make sure no one was watching, he scurried over to the trash can. He deftly lifted the lid and snatched two of the burnt loaves off the top of the pile, hoping these were slightly less germ-ridden than those further down. Returning the lid without a sound, he sat down with his back to the brick wall of the alley to enjoy his spoils.

The two loaves were badly blackened on the tops, but the majority of the bread was edible. In fact, to a man who hadn't eaten in nearly 48 hours, it was downright delicious. Matthew wolfed down the first one in seconds, then slowed down a bit to savor the second. Against all odds, he found himself completely at peace just then. The sun was warming despite the cool air, he had food in his belly and his clothes had nearly dried out. There was nothing about work to cause him stress, nor about his family. His problems didn't exist yet. They wouldn't for decades.

Of course, he was aware of the fact that this was not a sustainable lifestyle. He couldn't sleep in Central Park forever, venturing out only to hunt for food from trash cans like a raccoon. Until he found some way to get back to the time period he'd come from, which he wasn't even sure was possible, he was going to need to establish a more civilized routine. He needed a bed, and clean clothes, and maybe even meals that hadn't already been discarded by others. But to obtain any of those things, he would need money. And to get money, he needed a job.

Matthew was not sure of all the jobs that existed in 1919, but he was pretty confident that he would not be able to find work as a high-powered consultant in this day and age. He'd spent so many years educating himself and building up his skills in economics and business, and now he was a homeless bum. And, to the people around him, an immigrant. Skilled labor was not much of an option for those of his new social status. He'd heard that term a lot in high school history classes, "skilled labor." But in reality, he wasn't exactly sure what skilled or unskilled meant in the context of Manhattan in the early 20th century. He could read and write, and add and multiply, but he'd never worked with his hands, or experienced the challenges of surviving on minimum wage.

As he chewed thoughtfully on the blackened bread, Matthew looked out into the city street for potential inspiration. An elderly man with pinstriped suspenders hobbled past, reminding Matthew of a professor he'd had back at Dartmouth. Professor Garrison had been teaching introductory economics for years, pressing on long after most of his colleagues had retired. He wheezed for breath mid-lecture, taking breaks to lean against the chalkboard and rest. Once, a student had asked him why he continued teaching instead of retiring and moving someplace warm and tropical.

"Why would I ever stop doing what I love?" Garrison had replied.

At the time, Matthew had shaken his head and smiled at what he took for a lovably senile old man. Now, remembering the incident, he found himself thoroughly puzzled. *What do I love?* The question was so simple, so fundamental, that he was shocked when he could not find the answer. All he knew was that he had never felt toward consulting what Professor Garrison felt toward teaching freshmen about supply and demand.

As a shadow passed over Matthew, a warm, musical voice brought him back to reality.

"Every-ting okay dere, meester?"

Matthew looked up to see a short, portly Italian man standing before him, blocking the sun. The man had a thick black mustache and hair, and wore a white double-breasted jacket over checkered pants, along with a tall white chef's hat. In the crook of one arm he carried a large woven basket full of fresh vegetables. His dark eyes twinkled with concern as he looked down at the disheveled scavenger before him.

"Oh, I'm fine, thank you!" Matthew replied.

The Italian man gave a relieved smile and a small nod and started to turn to continue on his way. But before he had fully spun, he hesitated, and turned back toward Matthew.

"You need some-ting to eat, no?"

Matthew blushed, suddenly self-conscious of his appearance.

"Oh, I'll be alright, sir!"

The Italian man smiled again, but seemed unconvinced.

"You come-eh with me, meester!" He leaned over and extended a hand to help Matthew up to his feet.

He didn't understand the little man's insistence, but it was the first show of genuine friendliness he had experienced in this past reality, and he was not about to pass it up. He took the Italian's outstretched hand and pulled himself off the ground. His legs ached as he stood, and he found he was quite stiff from his night in the park. Brushing the dirt from the seat of his pants, he took a deep breath and steadied himself for his next adventure.

Chapter 6

The Italian man smiled warmly, his cheeks flushed and his eyes dancing. He patted Matthew on the back reassuringly, then extended an open hand toward the city street, indicating their path. The two began walking along in the rejuvenating sunlight.

"My name-eh ees Carlo," the Italian said in his smooth, rolling accent.

"I'm Matthew. Nice to meet you."

"You are new here, no?"

Matthew chuckled and paused for a moment to consider the question.

"I've been here before, but not for a very long time."

Carlo nodded enthusiastically and chattered on, pointing out different streets and stores and churches to his new friend. He was a few inches shorter than Matthew's 5'10" frame, but nearly twice as wide, with stocky legs and a full, round stomach. He was made wider by the big basket of vegetables he carried at his side. Despite his heavyset build, he was light on his feet, dancing quickly along the sidewalk while he identified various landmarks to Matthew. His black hair and mustache had a few gray strands interspersed, and Matthew guessed that he was in his early 40s. The sleeves of the white jacket were rolled up a few times, as were the cuffs of his pants, to accommodate his shorter-than-average limbs. Beneath the dark hair on his forearms, there were a few shiny scars that seemed to be the result of burns.

Matthew had to walk quickly to keep up with the lively little chef, and he tried to commit to memory each of the locations that Carlo identified. Grand Central Station, the Met Life Tower, the Flatiron Building. They were landmarks that he had seen before in passing, but now he made a point of memorizing the front of each building and its exact position. They walked for over an hour, but the time seemed to fly as Matthew's cheery tour guide showed him the city.

Finally, the duo arrived in the area Matthew recalled to be Little Italy. It was bustling with people; men, women, and children alike. Muscular men in dirty coveralls and tattered caps carried on boisterous conversations as they made their way toward their construction jobs at locations throughout the city. Women in small groups laughed noisily as they ambled along buying groceries. Little boys in oversized hand-medowns chased each other down the street in the direction of Upper Manhattan, their bulky newspaper bags thumping against the backs of their legs.

Matthew took in the scene around him in dumbstruck wonder. He'd never been one for history classes as a child, but witnessing this moment in a past world was perhaps the most fascinating experience he had ever had. He didn't even realize he'd stopped walking until Carlo patted him gently on the back to bring him back to reality. The Italian said nothing, but gave an understanding smile. Matthew pulled himself together, nodded slightly, and the two continued on.

They arrived at their destination soon after. Only a short ways into the neighborhood of Little Italy, Carlo stopped and turned toward a protruding storefront with red and green striped awnings. On a dirty white sign hanging on the brick wall above the awning were the words "Il Giardino di Carlo" in graceful red letters. Matthew's Italian was very limited but he recognized the word "giardino." *Carlo's Garden.*

"This is your place? Carlo's Garden?" Matthew asked.

"Ees my restaurant-eh, si!" Carlo beamed proudly as he too looked up at the sign bearing his name.

"So you're the owner *and* the chef?"

"Yes yes! Me and my wife-eh, we open dees place-eh when we move here to America, twelve years ago!"

Matthew was impressed. He tried to imagine starting a business from scratch. He wondered what it would be like to see something grow from a tiny idea, a spark, into a full-fledged reality. When he looked back at Carlo, the little entrepreneur was still smiling.

"Are-eh you hungry, Matt-yoo?"

Chapter 7

Carlo politely held open the door, and Matthew stepped across the threshold into the restaurant. It was not a particularly large space, but it was well-organized and efficiently utilized. Simple but well-crafted wooden tables of various sizes were spread throughout the room, each adorned with plain reddish-gold linen tablecloth. There was a short but clean forest-green carpet on the floor, and the brick walls were painted a pleasant off-white.

Carlo led the way across the dining area, weaving deftly between the tightly packed tables back to a swinging saloon-style door that opened up to the restaurant's kitchen area. The walls were lined with steel counter, broken up by cast-iron combination gas ovens and stovetops. In one back corner was large divided sink basin with two faucet heads, and a few ragged towels hanging from the front. Pots and pans and cooking utensils filled one set of wooden shelves over the back counter, and simple white serving plates, bowls, and cups filled another. The floors and counters appeared freshly washed, and one of the side walls housed two doors.

Standing beside the sink was a skinny boy of perhaps twelve. He wore black pants that had clearly been shortened considerably, and a baggy white shirt with the sleeves rolled up past his elbows. His hands were damp from washing dishes, and he held a tattered dish towel. He had frozen midway through drying his hands, and looked up at the two men from beneath a mop of shiny black hair. His large, dark eyes considered Matthew carefully, but gave no trace of any emotion, positive or negative.

"Matt-yoo, dees ees my son, Massimo! Massi, say hello to Meester Matt-yoo!"

Matthew watched as the young Massi bowed his head slightly toward his father, then approached the stranger. He moved silently and quickly across the kitchen and stopped before Matthew. The dark eyes, flashing with something that struck Matthew as intelligence, glanced up to his visitor's face for just a moment before returning respectfully to the floor, as he extended a hand and spoke.

"It is nice to meet you, Mister Matthew." The boy's soft, clipped voice shared the same musical quality as his father's, but contained no trace of the heavy Italian accent.

"The pleasure's all mine, Massi!" Matthew couldn't help but smile at the boy as he retreated, cat-like, back to the sink to resume washing dishes. He was so respectful! So obedient! Carlo was watching Matthew's reaction and seemed to understand.

"Massi ees a very good boy," he said proudly. "He wash-eh the dishes and serve-eh the food. One day Massi will be the boss here." He turned back toward his diligent son. "Massi, ees mama back yet?"

"No, papa. I have not seen her return."

"Ah, well, Matt-yoo will have-eh to settle for no meat thees time." He smiled, setting the basket of vegetables down and rolling up his sleeves. Glancing over at Matthew, he explained, "My wife-eh, Isabella, buys de meat for de restaurant-eh each week from-eh the butcher Franco."

Matthew had no idea who Franco was, of course, but he nodded as if he understood completely. Carlo plucked a pot from the shelf and filled it about halfway with water. He lit the stove and set the pot down on it to heat up. He then strode over to one of the large doors and opened it, offering Matthew a glimpse of a small but well-organized and tightly packed storeroom. He returned with a small bag of flour and a glass bottle of olive oil and set them on the counter. Winking at Matthew as if to say *"Watch this!"*, Carlo turned his head to call back to his son.

"Hey, Massi!"

"Yes, papa?"

"You want-eh to help me cook for Meester Matt-yoo?"

The boy's guarded expression broke into an excited smile.

"Yes, papa!"

"Okay, well, you know what to do!"

Little Massimo scampered over to place the freshly scrubbed dishes on the shelf, then across the room to a small wooden coat hook where a few stained white aprons were hanging. His nimble fingers quickly located what was clearly his own personal tiny apron, and he tied it around his waist as he scurried back to the sink to wash his hands. He then darted to his father's side, looking up at him and awaiting directions. Carlo beamed.

"Massi ees learning to cook-eh the food! He want-eh to be a chef someday like-eh hees papa!" He looked down at his eager protégé. "Massi, *quattro uova, per favore!*"

While Massi fetched four eggs from the strange-looking refrigerator, Carlo made a pile of flour directly on the counter top, and picked out a small glass bowl and poured in a few tablespoons of the olive oil. Carrying the large eggs carefully in his thin fingers, Massi looked up with a hopeful expression. Carlo couldn't restrain a grin, and nodded. Delighted, the boy set the eggs down gently and pulled a trash pail over to where he was standing. With a look of total concentration, he cracked the first egg against the edge of the counter and dumped its contents into the bowl of olive oil. As he continued with the remaining three eggs, his hands shook slightly but not a single piece of eggshell ended up in the bowl.

Carlo gave the oil and eggs a quick stir, then made a well in the pile of flour and poured in the mixture. He then proceeded to stick his bare hands into the well, further mixing the oil and eggs and slowly incorporating more and more of the flour. His hands made quick, precise circles, and Matthew found himself mesmerized watching. At his side, little Massi was mesmerized, too.

Once the dough was combined, Carlo began kneading it. His familiarity with his culinary medium reminded Matthew of musicians or dancers, who could lose themselves so completely in their craft, to whom the creative and the profound seemed to come naturally. The minutes slipped by and not a word was spoken.

Once he was satisfied, Carlo placed a clean bowl over the ball of dough to let it rest. Massi took this as his cue and immediately began to clean up the excess flour on the counter, while Carlo examined his collection of fresh vegetables. He selected three small onions and a head of garlic, removing four cloves. After quickly dicing the onions and garlic with a sharp knife, he deftly scraped them into a saucepan and added a drizzle of olive oil, setting the pan on the stove beside the now-bubbling pot of water.

Carlo began to reach for the vegetables again, then paused and glanced down at his son. Massi was watching astutely, his wide dark eyes carefully observing his father's every move. Carlo smiled and nudged him with his elbow. He nodded toward the basket, and Massi grinned. He walked over to the vegetables and peered into the basket, his chin just clearing the brim. His small, nimble fingers rifled through the produce, selecting fresh carrots, celery stalks, and plenty of ripe red tomatoes. Carlo set to work dicing the celery and carrots to sauté in the saucepan, and gave the tomatoes a rough chop in a small bowl, saving the juices. Meanwhile, Massi darted off to the storeroom and retrieved a few sprigs of parsley and a couple of bay leaves.

The crushed tomatoes and herbs went into the saucepan as well, along with some salt and pepper, and Matthew felt his stomach rumbling as he smelled the sauce cooking. Carlo turned down the heat on the stove a bit and returned to the dough he'd prepared earlier. Dabbing his hands in the leftover flour, he gave the dough a quick knead and then set it down on the counter. Massi scurried away for a moment and returned with a large wooden rolling pin, which he handed to his father. Carlo rolled the dough repeatedly until it was a thin sheet, which he sliced into delicate strands of spaghetti. He then gathered the freshly-made pasta and dropped it into the boiling water on the stove.

Carlo stepped back, brushing the remaining flour off of his hands. Matthew realized no one had spoken since the cooking began. Another rumble from his stomach, audible this time, broke the silence. The corners of Massi's mouth turned upward and Carlo chuckled warmly.

"You are-eh hungry, Matt-yoo! Ees okay, lunch-eh will be ready soon." He extended one hand toward the swinging door to the dining room, gesturing for Matthew to lead the way. As the two men entered the dining room, Massi darted to the back wall of the kitchen to fetch three plates, three glasses, and an assortment of utensils. He balanced the glasses carefully on top of the plates along with the silverware, and moved quickly but deliberately to a small table in the corner of the dining room, where he set down the flatware and began arranging the place settings.

Carlo pulled out a chair for Matthew with a courteous nod, and Matthew sat, a bit flustered by the politeness. Wordlessly, the little Italian man held up one finger, and disappeared back into the kitchen. He returned with a pitcher of water, which he poured into the three glasses. He then turned to his son, who had finished arranging the dishes and silverware.

"Massi, please-eh take care of Meester Matt-yoo while Papa finishes lunch-eh."

Massi bowed his head respectfully and sat down across from Matthew, and Carlo strolled happily away. Matthew watched him go, then turned back toward the child before him. Massi said nothing, but silently evaluated him with dark, almond-shaped eyes. Matthew shifted uncomfortably in his seat. He'd never been great with kids. He liked them, sure, but he always felt awkward and unsure around them. How was he supposed to behave? What was he supposed to talk about, anyway? Hesitatingly, he cleared his throat.

"So, Massi... Um... When did you start cooking with your father?"

"My eleventh birthday," the boy answered quietly. His eyes never wavered from Matthew's face. "Papa says by the time I'm thirteen I'll be able to help out in the kitchen full-time. He says people don't like their food made by a boy, but when I'm thirteen I'll be a man."

"And when will that be?" Matthew inquired.

"In ten months. I turned twelve in September."

"Do you want to run the restaurant when you're all grown up?"

Massi nodded modestly.

"Yes, Mister Matthew. Someday it will be my job to take over the restaurant. I will make Mama and Papa proud."

Matthew tried to think back to when he was Massi's age. As a boy, he'd often spend his time daydreaming and drawing sketches in his notebook. His father felt he should have been using the time for debate clubs and Latin classes, the better to prepare for law school one day. For a while, Matthew had gone along with his father's wishes, allowing himself to be shuttled to and from various resume- and skill-building activities in preparation for a lifetime of boredom at his father's law firm. As he grew older, however, he began to resent the lack of freedom and choice, and started taking courses in what interested him. He knew that there was no career for him in art, though, and eventually decided to study finance and strategy soon after he graduated from Dartmouth.

"Mister Matthew?" He snapped back to reality to see the boy looking quizzically up at him.

"Yes, Massi?"

"Where do you work? You don't dress like Papa."

Matthew wasn't quite sure how to answer that one.

"Well… I'm not from around here, actually. I'm from a place far away. But when I was there I worked with people to help them decide how to invest their money."

"What's 'invest'?"

"Investing is when you buy something and hope that you can sell it for more than you paid for it. People sometimes invest so that they can make more money."

Massi frowned, confused.

"But what if you can't sell the thing for more than you paid?"

"Well that's the problem. Investing is a risk. Sometimes you might have to wait a long time before the selling price goes up. Sometimes it never goes up. So it's possible to lose money too. There's no guarantee that you'll turn a profit."

"Why do people do it if they lose money sometimes?"

"They're hoping to make money. They hire people like me to help them decide what is most likely to make them money."

Massi nodded slowly, beginning to understand.

"But how do you know which things are good and which things are bad?"

"Well, we never know for sure. But we study the patterns and figure out what options are most likely to be best for a particular client."

"What's a client?"

"A client is the person or group that hires me. Kind of like the customers at your dad's restaurant."

"So is that what you wear for your work? Like Papa's apron?"

Matthew looked down at his outfit. His jeans and blue-and-white-striped button-down shirt were muddy and wrinkled. He chuckled.

"Not exactly. Usually I would wear nicer clothes. And certainly cleaner. I've just had a rough couple of days, so I'm not dressed for work."

"When do you have to work? Papa works every day."

Matthew opened his mouth, then closed it, unsure of how to respond. Would he be back working at the firm in a week? In a month? Ever? Thankfully, Carlo bustled back into the room just then, saving Matthew from having to answer.

"Lunch-eh ees served!" the Italian boomed. One arm held a large white bowl full of steaming pasta, tossed in a thick red marinara sauce. In the other was a bowl containing a leafy green salad, the vegetables shiny with a simple oil-and-vinegar dressing. He set both bowls on the table, topped off Matthew and Massi's water glasses, then sat down in the empty chair. The rich aromas of the food made Matthew's mouth water.

"Carlo... This looks incredible!"

Carlo smiled and served his guest a generous portion of pasta and salad. He then filled Massi's plate, and finally his own. He motioned for Matthew to begin eating. Matthew didn't need to be told twice.

The vegetables were fresh and crisp, the pasta firm and satisfying, and the sauce zesty and flavorful. He had wolfed down nearly half his plate before he looked up, embarrassed, and set down his fork. Massi was grinning at him through a forkful of pasta from across the table. Matthew took a gulp of water and cleared his throat.

"Everything is absolutely delicious, Carlo!"

Carlo beamed and patted his round stomach.

"Ees just an old-eh family recipe."

"It's the best pasta I've ever had."

Carlo laughed, shaking his head.

"Just wait, Meester Matt-yoo! When I have-eh more time-eh I will make you some-ting much more exciting."

The trio continued their meal, each eating their fill and then leaning back and enjoying their nice full bellies. For a few minutes no one spoke. Massi then rose and began collecting the used dishes, stacking them carefully and carrying them back to the kitchen. Matthew started to stand up to help, but Carlo set a hand on his arm.

"Seet, Matt-yoo. Massi will take-eh care of the deeshes."

Matthew did as instructed and sat back down.

"I can't thank you enough for this Carlo. How can I repay you?"

Carlo held up a hand and shook his head.

"You do not owe me a ting, Matt-yoo. Ees my pleasure to help a man in need."

The two men were silent for a moment as Massi returned to clear off the remaining dishes. Carlo was giving Matthew a funny look.

"Do you have a job, Matt-yoo?"

"Um… I did. I used to. But I guess I don't anymore…"

"Do you have a place to live?"

Matthew squirmed uncomfortably. Central Park wasn't exactly a home address.

"Not at the moment, no…"

Carlo pondered this for a moment, sizing up his homeless, unemployed guest.

"Perhaps you could stay weet us for a few days, unteel you find a place-eh to live?"

"Oh, I couldn't do that Carlo. You've already done more than enough; I couldn't impose on you like that."

"Nonsense, Matt-yoo. We all need help some-eh-times."

Matthew felt a bit uncomfortable faced with such generosity. However, the prospect of a soft, warm bed, and maybe even a shower, was too tantalizing to pass up.

"Carlo, that would be wonderful. But I can't just take advantage of your hospitality. Is there something I can do to earn my keep?"

Carlo scratched his head as he thought about a task for Matthew.

"Hmm… Ah, you can work weet Massi! You can wash deeshes and help around the restaurant-eh. We have an extra room in our apart-a-ment-eh upstairs."

Matthew was speechless. He was afraid if he opened his mouth to speak, he just might start crying with relief. Carlo stood and placed his hand gently under Matthew's arm, helping him to his feet. He led the way to a door near the entrance to the kitchen, opening it to reveal a tight staircase. At the top of the stairs, he opened another door to enter a small apartment. At the end of a narrow hallway, Carlo stopped in front of an open doorway.

"Dees ees the spare-eh room. There ees a bathroom down the hall. Make-eh yourself at home and get some rest. You can help Massi weet the dinner rush tonight."

Carlo excused himself to begin preparing for the evening's work. Matthew walked into the tiny room, which contained a bed, a mirror, and a small dresser with a lamp. It was better than the nicest hotel he'd ever seen. He peered out a dirty window at the city street two stories below, then made his way down the hall to the bathroom. He found a clean towel in the closet beside the bathroom, and brought it with him. The shower faucet squealed as water started to flow. Matthew shed his clothes and stepped into the shower without allowing it to heat up, gasping as the cold drops struck his skin. He washed his hair, then his body, then stood for a minute to simply enjoy the sensation of being clean.

Matthew pulled back the curtain and reached for the soft green towel. As he dried himself off, he noticed a neatly folded set of clothing on the counter beside the sink. Carlo must have left them there for him. Matthew first pulled on the off-white underwear and thick gray socks. The gray trousers were a good length, but far too wide in the waist. Thankfully, a set of well-worn black suspenders lay beside the clothes. He donned the white baggy undershirt and button-down, and then struggled with the suspenders for a few minutes before securing them to the trousers. He plucked a comb from beside the sink and ran it through his hair, hung up the towel on a rack next to the shower, and strolled back to the spare bedroom.

Matthew folded his dirty clothes neatly and set them atop the dresser to wash later. He turned out the lamp, letting the afternoon sunlight dimly illuminate the room. Sitting down on the bed, he was unable to suppress a deep sigh. He lay back, clean and warm and full and comfortable, and let his eyelids drift shut. He was asleep in seconds.

Chapter 8

The familiar tropical breeze. Soft white sands beneath his feet. The crystal blue waters and reassuring heat of the sun. Matthew was standing this time, enjoying the view of the seemingly endless ocean. The air was so clear and the water so calm that he could see for miles, so far that he could make out the curvature of the earth on the horizon. The warm rays of sunlight seemed to rejuvenate him, restoring his strength. He stretched out his arms above his head, tilting his head back to soak up as much of the warmth as possible.

A soft sound captured his attention. A short, repetitive thump. It came in three's, with a long pause in between. He scanned the beach for the source of the noise, but found nothing. Nor did the gently-lapping waters provide any clues. The thumping became a bit louder, a bit more insistent.

Matthew opened his eyes slowly, fighting the return to consciousness. He wanted to drift back into his dream, back to the beautiful sandy shores of the Jamaica of his imagination. He heard the three soft thumps, and for a moment he thought he had successfully re-entered the dream. However, as the room around him continued to materialize, he faced up to the reality that he was indeed awake. As the thumping began once more, he finally realized that the noise was someone knocking patiently on the door to his new room.

Sitting up in his bed, he rubbed at his eyes and paused briefly to steady himself. The room was spinning in a way that suggested to Matthew he had been deep in sleep. He eased himself onto the creaky wooden floor, and shuffled over to the door. Opening it, he found Massi standing on the other side. The boy's hair had been combed neatly, and he was dressed identically to Matthew, in a baggy white button-down and gray trousers held up by suspenders.

"Papa said to wake you", he said. "It's almost time to open the restaurant. Are you ready?"

Matthew scratched his head groggily and remembered he was to help Massi with his responsibilities to pay his rent while he stayed with the generous Italian family.

"Right! Yes. I'm ready." He smoothed out the wrinkles in his shirt and trousers, slipped on his shoes, and followed Massi back through the apartment and down the stairs to the restaurant. They headed directly into the kitchen, where Carlo was slicing a huge sheet of pasta dough. A short, slender woman stood beside him, dicing fresh vegetables. She had tan skin, dark hair, large brown eyes and full red lips. She appeared to be in her early 40s, with a few stray gray strands scattered amongst her sleek black hair. She and Carlo both looked up as Massi and Matthew entered the room, and Carlo beamed.

"Here-eh they are! The two finest deeshwashers in-eh the world!"

Massi rolled his eyes and smirked, and Matthew embarrassed himself by blushing as the beautiful woman at Carlo's side looked up and met his eyes. Seeing this, Carlo chuckled.

"Very beautiful, no? I am a lucky man. Matt-yoo, meet Isabella. Bella, meet Matt-yoo."

Matthew did nothing for a moment, then lurched forward to shake Isabella's hand, nodding his head politely.

"Nice to meet you, Matthew," she said with a radiant smile. Her accent was much less pronounced than her husband's.

"The pleasure's all mine, Miss Isabella."

"Please, call me Bella."

Carlo and Bella returned to their dinner preparations, chatting quietly in musical Italian as they did so. Massi tugged on Matthew's sleeve and gestured for him to follow. Doing as he was instructed, Matthew soon found himself in the storeroom in the back of the kitchen. There, Massi pointed out where he could find the flour, salt, herbs, oils, vegetables, and anything else Carlo might ask for during the rush. He also identified the meat and cheeses in the refrigerator, as well as the spare pots, pans, and cooking utensils. After the tour, the unlikely duo retrieved tall stacks of glasses and small bread plates from the shelves at the back wall, and set the tables in the dining room. Matthew watched his young tutor carefully, doing his best to emulate him exactly.

As they arranged the napkins and silverware artfully around each place setting, two muscular young men in neat black slacks and white button-downs entered the restaurant. They both wore shiny black shoes and had their dark hair gelled back. The pair appeared to be in their early twenties, and looked quite alike. Seeing them enter, Massi smiled and set down the napkin he'd been folding. He darted through the tables to the two men, who embraced him in a group hug.

"*Come stai, fratello?*" The three exchanged jokes and playful punches on the arm before they remembered Matthew was in the room. Massi led the two men over to his new dishwashing partner. He tilted his head back to look up at them.

"This is Matthew. He works here now. He's staying in the apartment with us for a while and he's going to help me wash dishes." Turning to Matthew, he continued, "And these are my two older brothers. Federico and Renato. They both do construction work during the day, but they help out here as waiters at night."

Matthew shook hands with the brawny brothers, who seemed quite friendly and accepting of the stranger who was now living with their family. Renato, the eldest, was 24 and lived with his wife and infant son in an apartment a few blocks over. Federico, at 22, was a bit taller, and had a scar on one cheek from a construction accident. He had just married a few months earlier, and also lived with his wife, on the same street as Renato. Just then, the loud ringing of a bell drew their attention towards the kitchen. Carlo stuck his head out the door and smiled.

"Good, Matt-yoo, you have-eh met the rest of *la famiglia*! Ees show-time, boys!"

Renato strode towards the wooden podium where the menus were kept, and stood straight and tall behind it, the picture of service and class. Federico walked straight to the door to the restaurant and opened it, letting in a small stream of customers who had been waiting eagerly outside. Massi led Matthew back into the kitchen, where they set to work washing pots and cutting boards that Carlo and Bella had used in their preparations, so that they could be used again later if necessary without any contamination.

In the beginning, things were pretty slow. Federico and Renato would bring back slips of paper with the customers' orders on them and Carlo would set to work preparing the dishes, with Bella as his more-than-capable sous chef. As the night went on, though, the pace picked up and soon it was all Matthew could do to follow what was happening. The family shouted back and forth to one another in the now-hectic kitchen in a mixture of English and Italian.

"Two pollo parmigiano!"

"Si, two chicken parmesan, coming up!"

"Is the spaghetti marinara ready?"

"On the counter, si!"

"Where ees the sugar?"

"Ecco lo zucchero!"

72

And then, as quickly as it had started, the rush ended. At first, Matthew didn't even realize. He just knew that for the first time in hours he seemed to be catching up on the stack of dirty dishes to his left, finally making a dent before the clean dishes were swept away back into the dining room. He was only made aware otherwise when Renato and Federico strolled into the kitchen, clapping one another on the back and laughing loudly. Glancing up, he saw that Massi had set down the plate he was drying.

Carlo gestured for the dishwashers, the waiters, and his sous chef to join him at the counter, where he was pouring six small glasses of red wine. As they each picked up a glass, Carlo looked around and smiled.

"A toast, to another wonderful night with family…" he paused, and looked over at Matthew. "And with new friends."

Matthew tipped back his glass, letting the wine warm his face and the family his heart.

Chapter 9

As the days passed, Matthew adjusted quickly to his new life and new routine. He woke early each morning to accompany Carlo on his vegetable runs, helped clean around the apartment during the day, and assisted Massi with washing the dishes and helping around the restaurant. Like Massi, he quickly took an interest in the culinary arts, and Carlo included him in his son's introductory cooking lessons when there was free time.

The days became weeks, and the weeks became months. The seasons changed, and a new Matthew was born. He had a new home, a new family, a new job. He rarely thought about his old life in the next millennium, and when he did, it wasn't for long because it made his head hurt. In no time at all, he advanced through the ranks of the small family business, and soon became Carlo's assistant chef. Bella shifted over to waitressing and making small talk with the customers, a position she much preferred due to the social aspects.

Matthew had never done much cooking in his past life, at least not beyond the usual cooking-for-survival bachelor style. Yet he found that it was a skill he adopted readily, inspiring Carlo to remark often that he was *"il naturale!"* He lost himself in cooking, totally immersed in the strange and wonderful world of textures and tastes, of aromas and colors. There were still rules to be followed, basic techniques and protocols that had to be obeyed, but there was also pure, unbridled imagination. Carlo granted him the freedom to experiment with dishes in his time off, and when Matthew felt he had something special, he could have the master chef try it out. Soon enough, Carlo was adding new appetizers to the menu.

Perhaps it was the newfound confidence in his cooking abilities, or perhaps it was the freedom of being dropped into a world where no one knew him, but Matthew found himself opening up socially as well. He struck up conversations with strangers in the street on his way to buy groceries, even though some of them were rude to him just on the basis of his race. He learned the names of the employees at his favorite stores, barber shops, and theaters. And he also made a point to get to know the restaurant's regulars, whenever possible.

Unlike the old Irishman he'd met at the tavern his first night in the city, the Italians seemed to accept the new Korean chef with open arms. The restaurant's patrons were friendly and warm, and were not the least bit bothered by Matthew's ethnicity. After all, the man could prepare an excellent chicken marsala!

Matthew took a special liking to a few customers in particular. There was the Aiello family, who came in each Saturday without fail for a family dinner. Then there were Mr. and Mrs. Filipipi, an elderly couple who always tipped well and brought a few sweets from their shop for Massi. But the diner who most intrigued Matthew was a woman who came in a few times each month, and often with a male guest, although not always the same one. Every time he saw her, she had on a hat. But no simple, run-of-the-mill hat. She was always wearing some sort of funny, colorful piece, always coordinated perfectly with her outfit. For a while, Matthew was too intimidated to approach her.

One rainy Thursday evening, though, when business was slow, Matthew decided to introduce himself. He had to meet this woman. She was wearing a scarlet wide-brimmed hat with a shiny violet feather over her sleek, immaculate raven-colored hair. The hat was tipped quite precariously on her head but did not fall, and the violet of the hat matched the silk flowers embroidered elegantly into the back and sleeves of her fitted gray dinner jacket.

Peering through the kitchen door into the dining room, Matthew saw that the mystery woman was alone, which was unusual for her. He wasn't sure how to approach her, finding her much more perplexing than the average customer. Taking advantage of the lull in activity in the kitchen, he quickly through together a small plate of bruschetta, arranging the dish as artfully as possible. He then brushed the crumbs from his apron and smoothed his shirt, then walked gracefully into the dining area. Reaching the woman's table in the corner, he carefully set down the bruschetta. She looked up from the book she was reading, examining Matthew from the corner of her eye.

"Compliments of the chef," he said as smoothly as possible.

She examined him for a long moment, saying nothing. Finally she spoke.

"What's your name, Mister?"

"I'm Matthew, ma'am."

"Well Matthew, why don't you sit down for a spell. As you can see, I'm in need of some company this evening."

Matthew was caught off-guard, but did as she asked. Settling into the chair across from her, he cleared his throat.

"I, uh, I like your hat. It's very nice."

She smiled a wry smile, and Matthew got the feeling that her piercing brown eyes could see straight into his soul.

"You're quite the chef, you know," she said.

"How did you know I'm a chef?" he asked.

She smirked.

"I'm not blind. I notice things. I've seen you through the kitchen door a few times. I know you started as a dishwasher, but the addition of the apron a few months back means you've graduated to cooking, correct?"

He nodded, impressed by the seemingly aloof woman.

"I'm still learning the ropes… But Carlo is a great teacher and he gives me a lot of room to experiment."

"Good. I've always thought experimentation was the best way to learn a trade. To be creative, and define your own style…" The mysterious woman trailed off, her eyes focusing intently into empty space.

Matthew shifted a bit in his chair, unsure of how long he should remain at the table. He certainly didn't want to overstay his welcome with this enigmatic customer. As if she could read his mind, the woman with the hat snapped back to reality and shook her head gently.

"I apologize. I get a bit lost in thought sometimes." She narrowed her eyes, sizing up her guest. "But I imagine you can relate, as a creative type yourself? I believe the best ideas come from that space between consciousness and dreaming."

For a moment, Matthew wasn't sure how to respond. It seemed such an odd topic of conversation to be discussing with someone he had just met. But he was excited, as the woman had described quite simply the phenomenon he'd been struggling to put into words for months.

"Exactly! That place where you're only barely aware of the world around you, and you're seeing connections that you would miss if you were too clear-headed!"

There was a silence, and Matthew began to worry that he had put off the mystery woman with his sudden enthusiasm. But after a long moment, the corners of the woman's mouth pulled upward in an approving smile.

"You are going to do big things, my dear." She extended a bony, graceful hand, thin metal bracelets clinking softly at her wrist. "I'm Adelina Bianchi. It's nice to meet you, Matthew."

Chapter 10

It was a good thing that business was slow that evening, because Matthew completely lost track of time sitting and chatting with Ms. Bianchi, or "Biani", as she'd asked him to call her. He learned that she was born and raised in Italy, and had then moved to London for a few years. There, she had met her husband, a medical doctor named Gerald. He was leading a lecture that she attended and, after a brief courtship, the two had moved to New York City. Gerald did not particularly like the city, however, and so she now saw him only occasionally when he came to visit. The arrangement struck Matthew as odd, especially for the time period, but then Biani did not seem the least bit concerned about convention in any aspect of her life.

She'd become interested in fashion after creating a ballgown out of a length of blue fabric in response to a late-notice invitation to a ball in Paris. Since then, she'd toyed with different designs and materials in her own wardrobe, modifying and embellishing store-bought items as well as creating a few from scratch. Now, she was working with a friend named Alesia Cattanio in a small boutique, selling French fashion items. One day, she said, she would move to

Paris and start her own line, to compete with the famed Emma De Fiore. She spoke plainly and bluntly about these plans. They were not a possibility. They were an as-of-yet-unrealized fact.

Matthew was mesmerized by Biani's stories of her peculiar and jet-setting life. There wasn't a single piece of information that wowed him particularly, but rather the whole picture. She was not a businessperson blindly following the next dollar, she was an artist, twirling and dancing ever forward. Her experiences just seemed so *interesting*. By contrast, his own seemed painfully dull, and he struggled with how to respond when she asked him about his life.

"I… well, you see… uhmm… it's kind of hard to explain… I guess-"

Biani laughed out loud at his sudden discomfort.

"Well I didn't mean to put you on the spot! Let's start with the basics. Where are you from?"

"California. Well, New Jersey as well, ma'am."

"Don't call me ma'am, I'm not old enough for that yet. And what brought you to the Big Apple? All of the employment opportunities in the Italian cuisine industry?"

Matthew laughed, then fell silent. How exactly *did* he get here?

"Well... I guess I was visiting some old friends. Then I just ended up staying longer than I'd planned. Carlo offered me a job and lets me stay in the spare room, so that's how I got to this restaurant, specifically."

Biani nodded, considering his story.

"Carlo is a good man. I've been visiting this restaurant regularly since I came to New York, and he's always been wonderfully friendly. Quite the chef, too! The whole family is terrific."

"They really are! I could never repay them for their generosity."

"And I've seen you spending a lot of time with the youngest boy, too, right?"

"Yes ma'am. Sorry, Biani! Massimo is a great kid... not to mention a better chef than me!"

Biani laughed warmly.

"I don't doubt that he's quite the chip off the old block, but don't sell yourself short, Matthew. You're more talented than you realize."

The words struck Matthew like a ton of bricks. He didn't know how to respond. Biani tilted her head and narrowed her eyes as she watched him struggle to find the words.

"That's… I… I mean… I think that's the nicest thing anyone's ever said to me."

Biani's face broke slowly into a sad smile.

"I take it your parents weren't particularly warm, either, then."

"You could certainly say that, yes… It's just that my father is so successful, you know? Everything comes easily to him. But I'm not like that. I'm not like him. I'll never be able to relate to having everything seem so simple. And he doesn't seem to understand that I'm not as smart as he is, so I'm constantly disappointing him."

The words rushed out before Matthew could he could censor them. At the end of his brief tirade, he looked up at Biani, terrified that he had put her off irreparably. But her expression was one of understanding, not distaste. After a moment of consideration, she spoke, in a slow, measured cadence.

"Matthew, I think you might be mistaken about your father's ease in life. I would bet everything I own that he struggles with many aspects of life, be they professional or domestic, just like you and me and everyone else. I don't doubt that he's successful, but you've also probably built him up and idolized him beyond that. Which is natural, as he is your father. Everyone views their parents as something more than just people. And I assure you he's not disappointed in you. Not really. Parents just want their children to be the best they can be. Your father probably wants to help steer you to be more than he could ever be, and to try to eliminate certain behaviors of his own that he sees in you. I've dealt with the same insecurities my entire life. A few years back, I was experimenting with poetry. I published a book that was apparently a little too carnal for my parents' taste, and they sent me to a convent! And they still don't approve of my marriage to Gerald. It was a source of a lot of resentment for a long while, but I've come to accept that they do what they do because they care about me. So trust me, with a son as kind and intelligent and respectful as you, there is no chance that your father is disappointed."

Matthew felt a wave of emotion wash over him. He'd spent his entire life feeling like he had let his father down, and now Biani's words sliced into this core belief of his.

"I don't know. I'm not sure if it's the same. All my life, I've tried to do what he wants me to do. I studied hard, went to a top school, got an office job. And I can't stand that life. Honestly, a few months of being an assistant chef has been more rewarding than years spent at my last job. It's not even like I'm a great chef, either! I take twice as long as Carlo to prepare the same dish. Even Massi is faster than me, and he spends far less time practicing."

"Matthew, listen to me. Stop doing what you think your father expects you to do, and follow your own dreams. Don't be afraid of failure. There's no shame in falling on your face a few times if you're doing what you love. It seems to me that you're a free spirit. It's no surprise you weren't satisfied pushing paper all day. Stop repressing your innovative, inventive side. Be *persistently* creative. Maybe it's true that it takes you a bit longer than others to cook certain dishes. But, the food you create is more delicately prepared than most. That's just you, Matthew. You need to capitalize on your strong creativity, instead of obsessing over your lower output. What you do is an art, not a science."

As the words slowly sank in, Matthew began to smile. Biani grinned back, and for a while the two sat in pleasant silence, simply enjoying each other's company.

Chapter 11

The sun was breaking over the New York City skyline as Matthew and Carlo strolled briskly toward the market to collect vegetables for the day. It was the first warm day of spring, and Matthew basked in the sun, letting his body relax after months of stiff, shiver-inducing winter. Carlo whistled cheerfully as they walked, his round stomach bouncing jauntily with each step.

They reached the market, and wordlessly went their separate ways. Carlo set off to find tomatoes, celery, onions, mushrooms, and carrots. Matthew was in charge of procuring fresh herbs to season the dishes. He knew the best stalls to get fresh oregano, basil, majoran, fennel seeds, tarragon, rosemary, and thyme. He'd taken the same route through the market so many times that his mind was on autopilot.

Matthew met back up with Carlo at the edge of the market. They examined each other's selections approvingly. They began to walk back, chatting warmly about how nice it was to feel the sun, and how tall Massi was getting, and how sweet the Vincenti family was every time they came to visit the restaurant.

The conversation reached a natural lull, and Carlo turned to Matthew as the strolled.

"You know, Matt-yoo, there-eh ees some-ting I want to ask you."

"Of course, anything! What is it?"

"You have-eh been doing *molto bene* in the kitchen, and I tink you are-eh ready to move-eh on."

For one sick moment, Matthew felt his stomach drop. He'd known this day was coming, but he'd just pushed it out of his mind. It was time for him to stop living with Carlo and the family. He couldn't just stay with them indefinitely. Then Carlo continued speaking.

"I tink you should be-eh a full-time chef."

"Wait… so does this mean you're… promoting me?"

"*Si*, Matt-yoo! You cook very well!"

Matthew beamed like a child. There wasn't a huge age difference between the two men, but Matthew had come to view Carlo as something of a surrogate father figure, and the praise warmed his heart.

"Carlo, I'd be honored! I've really enjoyed learning to cook these past few months and I would love to take on some more responsibility in the kitchen."

"Of course, we will pay you more-eh as well."

"Oh no, I couldn't possibly accept a raise, Carlo! All that you do for me, letting me stay with the family, I could never take more money as well."

Carlo turned to consider Matthew again, examining his face carefully. Upon realizing that Matthew meant every word, and that he was entirely serious about not wanting any kind of monetary raise, he sighed.

"Well, Matt-yoo, eef you eensist. But you know, we love-eh having you stay weet us. Massi love-eh to have-eh you around! And you will be a beeg help during ze dinner rush."

"Well, thank you. It really does mean a lot to me to have somewhere to stay, and to have wonderful people around me every day. And I'm happy to help any way I can!"

"Great! You start-eh tonight."

Chapter 12

Electric. That was how Matthew felt working in the kitchen that evening. The work was fast-paced and exciting. He and Carlo were engaged in a kind of culinary dance, weaving around one another gracefully to the tune of Renato and Federico barking out orders from the dinner guests. Delectable smells filled the room, and the visual splendor of the food impressed him like never before. Carlo cracked jokes from time to time, and when Matthew glanced up, he could see Massi smirking over at the sinks, up to his elbows in soapy dishwater. Matthew didn't always catch enough of Carlo's rapid-fire Italian to understand what was being said, but the infectious, mischievous grin on Massi's face conferred the tone of the joke quite clearly.

Matthew was used to high-pressure work at the SB Finance, with strict deadlines and tense supervisors and endless phone calls and emails. But the dinner rush was a different kind of busy. It was a very sensory experience, a kind of physicality unlike anything he'd ever done before. He was using his brain, of course, but that wasn't all. The entire kitchen had become an extension of his body, and he found himself unusually aware of his presence in space. He was in tune with each of his five senses, his mind flooded with input from this rich environment. Perhaps the biggest difference between the restaurant and the firm, however, was the total absence of stress. Matthew could feel the time-sensitivity of his work, and wanted to serve each customer quickly, but it was a self-motivated pressure, free of anxiety.

Four hours seemed to pass in the blink of an eye. The rush ended, and Matthew found himself idle for the first time all evening. The blood coursing through his veins still felt electrified, and he turned eagerly to Carlo for further instructions.

"What's next? Should I prep more garlic bread or salad?"

Carlo chuckled and clapped Matthew on the back.

"No, Matt-yoo, dinner ees over. Now, we clean."

Even as he spoke, Renato and Federico swept into the kitchen, gracefully balancing stacks of dirty dishes in their arms as they exchanged good-natured barbs in a combination of English and Italian. They brought the dishes to the sink where Massi waited, then returned to the dining room with Carlo close behind to continue cleaning up. Matthew joined Massi at the sink and began enthusiastically scrubbing dishes, waiting for his high to slowly dissipate.

Bella glided into the kitchen after folding the tablecloths from the dining room. She came to stand beside Matthew and put away the dishes as he and Massi cleaned them. The trio worked in silence for a while. When they had finished, Bella turned toward Matthew and locked her dark, mysterious eyes on his.

"Carlo says you did very well today. He says you are a natural."

Matthew blushed in spite of himself, as usual a bit tongue-tied in response to the beautiful Italian woman's kind words. Massi noticed, and imitated Matthew's goofy, embarrassed expression. Matthew elbowed him in the ribs, and Massi giggled. Clearing his throat, Matthew turned back toward Bella.

"I'm glad he thought so. It was a wonderful experience for me too – I have a new respect for what you two do every day!"

Bella nodded demurely.

"We are very lucky to have this opportunity. It has given our family a new start."

She dabbed at the puddles of water around the sink with a dishtowel, leaving the area spotless.

"Okay, boys. Time for bed."

Chapter 13

It was about 4:00 PM. The dinner rush had not yet started, but a few patrons occupied the dining room, enjoying a late afternoon meal as the warm, slowly-setting sun slanted through the restaurant's windows. Matthew was standing towards the corner of the dining room, wrapping sets of silverware in cloth napkins. A sudden voice from behind startled him from his mindless reverie.

"So I hear you're a big-time chef now, huh?"

Matthew spun around to see Adelina Bianchi sitting at a small table just behind him. There was no food or drink at the table, no menus. It was just Biani, her hands on the table with fingers interwoven, sitting up straight but comfortably in her chair. She wore a long black skirt and a fitted magenta dinner jacket, embroidered elaborately with metallic gold thread. The embroidery formed a series of musical notes, which matched the music-note-shaped gold buttons on the jacket. Her head was hat-free, but instead bore a large decorative teal bow, offset on the side of her skull. The bow featured a number of small metallic music notes as well, and seemed to defy gravity floating a few inches above her left ear beside her tight, perfectly-smooth brunette bun.

Matthew smiled at the sight of his strange, stylish friend.

"You heard correctly. I got a promotion. Still don't know what I'm doing, of course, but I guess they trust me anyway."

Biani shrugged nonchalantly.

"None of us know what we're doing, darling. That's the adventure."

Matthew nodded, contemplating. He set down the rolls of silverware and walked over to her table, standing behind the empty chair opposite her.

"How are you doing, Biani?"

"I can't complain. The boutique is staying afloat, for now. I've got plenty of ideas for new designs, but I need an outlet. I can't stay here forever. My world's a bit too small right now. And how are you, Matthew?"

"I'm doing very well. Working as a full-time chef has been great!"

Biani was silent for a while, looking expectantly up at Matthew. He wasn't sure what she expected of him next. Finally she spoke.

"And?"

"And what?"

"What else?"

"I… I'm not sure I understand. What do you mean?"

She sighed, rubbing the bony fingers of one hand over the knuckles of the other.

"I mean, what else? What else is going on? What are your goals? Your next step? Where are you going from here? What will you accomplish next?"

Matthew frowned, considering her words.

"I guess I'm not really sure. I'm pretty happy with the way things are right now."

"And there's nothing wrong with being happy. But don't ever let yourself get complacent, Matthew. As soon as you settle for 'satisfied', or 'good enough', you cripple yourself. You cut off your potential for advancement. Stay hungry, stay ambitious, and the sky's the limit."

There was a long silence as the two stared at each other, reading hidden fears and aspirations in one another's eyes.

"Sit down, Matthew. I'm in need of some company. Let's chat."

Chapter 14

Matthew wasn't sure what exactly it was about Biani that made him so comfortable baring his soul. Maybe it was her remarkable ability to remain unfazed by anything and everything she heard. Maybe it was the way her dark eyes seemed to see right through him anyway. Or maybe it was the fact that she herself could share personal details of her life without so much as a flinch.

Whatever the reason, Matthew soon found himself telling Biani all about his love life, of all things. Or rather, his lack thereof. He hadn't been in a serious relationship in years, but he described his experiences dating while studying economics at Oxford. In London, he'd met women of all races, cultures, and builds. The cultural richness of the community had been eye-opening, and now he rarely paid attention to ethnicity or appearances, knowing these were not the traits that made people most interesting.

Biani had a hard time believing Matthew was an Oxford graduate. After all, she'd never met an Asian who had attended Oxford, and certainly not a poor Asian working in an immigrant Italian's restaurant. But Matthew had spoken of odd experiences before, and she had accepted his strange stories as one of his quirks. She was not one to judge another's unconventional life path.

Matthew had dated intermittently while at Oxford, but nothing had lasted very long. The women had been lovely, kind, and intelligent, but there was no spark. No passion. At times, Matthew admitted, he hated himself for his apparent inability to feel love for these perfectly wonderful ladies. To show the continuing deterioration of his love life, Matthew also wanted to explain his non-existent dating experience when he attended INSEAD, Europe's prestigious MBA program. He managed to stop mentioning it since he would sound lunatic if he talked about the French program that even did not exist in 1920s.

Biani shook her head.

"What did I just tell you Matthew? Don't be complacent. Don't be satisfied with 'nice enough' or 'compatible enough'. Set higher standards for yourself. Demand an extraordinary love."

"Have you found your extraordinary love with Gerald?"

Biani fell uncharacteristically silent.

"I thought I had. I was mistaken. I recently learned he's been having an affair."

Matthew's eyes widened and he instantly regretted asking the question.

"Oh no, Biani, I'm so sorry. It wasn't my business to ask."

She chuckled and waved one hand as if to brush away his silly words.

"Nonsense, darling, we're friends. Friends talk. Anyway, it's no matter. I have a new love of my life. My baby daughter, Yvonne. Regardless of what Gerald has done to wrong me, he gave me Yvonne, and for that I am grateful."

She paused for a moment, then smiled.

"Besides, it's not as if I'll be bringing him back to Paris with me. I've no room for dead weight. I'm asking for a divorce."

Her strength and calm in the face of such relationship turmoil astounded Matthew, and he aspired to someday be as fiercely self-assured and confidently independent as Biani.

Reading the admiration in his face, she reached out and took his hand.

"Be patient, Matthew. Don't fret. Keep striving, but don't force it. It's far better to be alone and happy than together and apathetic. You'll find your extraordinary someone someday, and when you do, you'll know. It will be clear. In the meantime, you are free. Other people have a tendency to tie you down and hold you back. But you are unchained."

Unchained. Matthew liked the sound of that. He'd always felt like he was supposed to follow the path of his father and so many others; get an education, get a job, meet a woman, get married, have kids, grow old. It wasn't exciting but it was familiar. Safe. Yet Biani's words stirred something deep within him. It was hope. Hope for something different, something unique, something fulfilling. Maybe he would meet the perfect woman eventually, but that was just one of many exciting moments to come. His life was an open book. He was free.

Chapter 15

Time marches on. Matthew was made painfully aware of this fact one morning as he and Carlo strolled to the market to collect vegetables. A young boy was selling newspapers on the street corner, and Matthew bought one on a whim. He read the date at the top, and gasped.

It was November 8, 1922. Three years had passed since the strange events of that fateful evening at his parents' house. Three years that he had lived in a different era, against all reason or logic.

He had changed a lot in those three years. He could scarcely remember the shy, passive, often resentful person he was when he had arrived in Central Park. He had evolved, grown, matured. He'd become a good friend to Carlo and Bella, and a big brother to Massi, who himself had sprouted into a fine young man.

Matthew had taken Biani's sage advice, and charged headfirst into living. He was now a well-known chef in Little Italy, and had his own section on the menu at Carlo's restaurant featuring his very own creations. His dishes were a huge hit and business was booming.

He'd also stayed hungry. He constantly wanted more, especially more creativity. He enjoyed crafting new meals and combinations of flavors, but he was ready for something new. He'd grown impatient with his quiet life as a chef. It wasn't that he didn't enjoy it. He enjoyed it immensely, and was grateful every day for the opportunity Carlo had given him. But there was also a gnawing emptiness, the sensation that somewhere, something more waited for him. He expressed these feelings to Biani over an early dinner that evening.

"It just… it feels like I've gotten everything I can out of this job, this life. I want to try something new, to be something different. But I can't do that here. I'm trapped."

Biani tilted her head, confused.

"Trapped how?"

"There's nothing left for me here. Not enough opportunities. I'm from a different world, where I can travel and do work in all sorts of fields and re-invent myself. I wish I could get back to that world."

Biani didn't understand why Matthew was always talking about this "other world", but she knew that it was hard for an immigrant, especially an Asian immigrant, to achieve much beyond a small business in this environment.

"I've been feeling a bit trapped myself, darling. That's actually why I wanted to have dinner tonight... I'm leaving tomorrow for Paris. I'm planning on opening my own boutique there."

Matthew blinked, speechless.

"Tomorrow? That's so… sudden."

Biani sighed and nodded. She reached across the table and took his hand reassuringly.

"I know, I know. I wanted to tell you earlier but I've been so busy making the arrangements, and you've been so busy with work that I didn't want to distract you."

"No, I understand, of course. And pardon me if this is out of place, but will Gerald be joining you in Paris?"

"You're not out of place at all, darling. I would hope you would know that. No, I believe this will be the end of the road for me and Gerald. We've no need for one another any longer."

Matthew hummed softly and took it all in for a moment. He was impressed as always by Biani's bravery and resourcefulness. It took guts in any decade to pick up and move your life across the globe, especially alone. But especially for a woman in this male-dominated world to travel and start a new chapter without male accompaniment, it was downright audacious.

"Will I ever see you again?" Matthew was a bit embarrassed by the way his voice broke mid-sentence.

Biani smiled sadly, her thumb running gently along the top of his hand.

"I can't say for certain, Matthew. I'm afraid I've no immediate plans to return to the States, and I've no way of knowing where exactly my new career may take me."

"So I suppose this is goodbye, then."

"I suppose it is. It's been truly wonderful getting to know you, darling. I do hope you'll remember me fondly." She gave his hand a last reassuring pat, and got to her feet to leave. Matthew leapt up, moving quickly to pull out her chair for her and help her with her coat. As she drew the coat around herself, she stopped suddenly.

"Oh! I'd almost forgotten. I have a parting gift for you, Matthew." She reached into her coat pocket and withdrew a small box wrapped neatly in green paper.

"What's this? I didn't have a chance to get you anything!"

Biani laughed and waved off his concern.

"Oh, please. Enough of that. Anyway, it's not much, just a trinket I noticed in passing last week. I thought it quite striking and thought perhaps it might grant you a bit of creative inspiration as well." She handed him the box and, to his surprise, drew him in forcefully for a hug.

After a long moment, Biani broke from the embrace, tipped her hat daintily towards Matthew, and strode out of the restaurant without another look back.

Chapter 16

The rest of the day passed slowly for Matthew. He had few friends in this world, and he feared losing one of them forever. The dinner rush, usually the highlight of his day, seemed to drag on without end. When finally the restaurant closed for the evening, and the family set to cleaning up, Carlo pulled Matthew aside, having noticed his glum mood.

"Why are you sad, Matt-yoo?"

"I'm sorry for moping, Carlo. My friend Biani is leaving for Paris tomorrow and I just found out this afternoon."

Carlo nodded sympathetically. He had seen Matthew conversing with the woman in the strange hats on multiple occasions, and knew the two were close.

"Do not worry about cleaning, Matt-yoo. Go out and have fun tonight."

Matthew wasn't sure what Carlo meant by fun, but he knew he wouldn't be of much use moving around like a zombie. The family would be able to clean up more quickly with him out of the way. Hanging up his apron, he drifted out to the street.

Now what? He thought. *Where am I supposed to go?* Feeling lost, he began to walk towards the center of the city. The chilly night air drew goosebumps from his skin, and he shivered. He passed block after block, on autopilot. Matthew wasn't sure how much time had passed when he found himself standing before the same rundown tavern he'd visited on his first night in 1919. Like a moth to light, he'd been drawn once more to the inviting warmth and music emitting from the door. *Why not? This place is as good as any.*

Ducking inside, Matthew made his way across the crowded floor, weaving in between enthusiastically swing-dancing couples. He reached the bar, ordered a beer, and settled in to drink, without making eye contact with any of the other patrons. He downed the beer more quickly than he knew was wise, and decided to switch to ginger ale to avoid outpacing his limits. All he wanted to do was clear his mind of stresses and concerns for a while, not make himself sick.

Midway through the ginger ale, Matthew was surprised by a tap on his shoulder. A thin white woman, with dark brown hair, gaunt features, and crooked teeth smiled broadly at him. Leaning in close enough that Matthew could smell the whiskey on her breath, she whispered in his ear.

"Wanna dance, mister?"

He let her lead him by the hand to the center of the crowded floor. There, she steered him expertly to and fro through the other couples, bouncing to the upbeat jazz filling the smoky air. His head was still swimming from the idea of losing Biani, and the swaying and spinning did nothing to help steady him. One song turned to two, and the night passed in a dizzying whirl of cigarette smoke and dancing. He was only dimly aware of what was happening when the tavern owner took him by the shoulders and guided him gently to the door. Looking around, he realized he and the gaunt-faced woman were a few of the last remaining patrons. She still clung to his arm as they stepped out into the chilly night air.

"Where to next, mister?" She grinned suggestively, and her face seemed to swirl before Matthew's eyes.

"I… I gotta get home. It was… It was very nice to meet you," he stammered. Dismayed, the woman sighed and walked away. Matthew stumbled home, exhausted. Eventually he reached the apartment, and trudged up the stairs and down the hall to his room. He kicked off his shoes and dropped his jacket on the floor. It made an unexpected thunk as it hit the ground, and he squinted down at it. He knelt to examine the jacket and noticed a large lump in the pocket. It was the gift from Biani.

Matthew removed the box and got to his feet. He tore off the neatly wrapped green paper, letting it fall to the floor. Inside was a small reddish brown wooden box. It creaked slightly as he opened it. A metallic glimmer reflected light from the lamp. As his vision cleared, Matthew discovered that the box's contents were a single delicate ring. A braided silver band inset with a deep red ruby. The same one he'd seen in his parents' backyard the night he'd collapsed.

Matthew suddenly grew very dizzy as the déjà vu hit him. Faster and faster, the contents of the room spun around him. The past three years whizzed by him in an instant, and then, without warning, the hard wooden floorboards rushed up to meet him, and the world was a deep, endless black.

Chapter 17

The soft crash of waves breaking gently on a sandy shore. The fronds of palm trees rustling quietly in response to a warm, seductive breeze. The sun warmed Matthew's bare chest as he reclined comfortably on a smooth cotton towel. He could smell the salty spray of the ocean in the air, mixed with the familiar scent of sunscreen. It seemed like the perfect place to stay forever, to simply lie in the tropical sun and give oneself completely over to relaxation.

But Matthew wasn't content with relaxation today. The breaking waves stirred in him a strange restlessness, a need to move, to explore, to create. He pressed off the silky sand and got to his feet. He looked first left, then right. There was nothing but sandy coastline as far as the eye could see. A vague sense of frustration began to gnaw at Matthew. He needed to be somewhere, doing something, but he could not identify where or what.

Turning around, he discovered that opposite the ocean, the beach ended at a thick green jungle. Lush emerald leaves the size of Matthew's head swayed gently in the draft of wind off the sea. Thick vines wound their way around gnarled tree trunks, and deep shadows obscured the world that waited beneath the leafy canopy. Like a magnet, Matthew found himself drawn towards the mysterious jungle.

Reaching the edge of the tropical forest, he paused only briefly, wracking his brain for a reason behind his actions. The soul-searching was short-lived, however, as the magnet drew him incessantly forward into the shadows. He picked his way carefully over the exposed roots and dense bushes as he ventured deeper and deeper into the jungle. Snakes slithered over branches, but he was not afraid. Monkeys hooted loudly and leapt between trees, but he was not distracted. A large, brightly colored parrot, however, captured his attention entirely.

The parrot cocked its head at Matthew as he approached. The bird's feathers were ruffled, and it shuffled a bit in place. Tilting its head to the other side, it opened its beak to squawk.

"Beep."

Matthew squinted at the parrot, confused. That wasn't the sound birds were supposed to make.

"Beep. Beep."

He was unable to reconcile the noise with the creature before him. The beeping became a steady, regular rhythm and Matthew grew uneasy.

"Beep. Beep. Beep. Beep."

Bright lights. That was the first thing Matthew noticed as his eyes fluttered open slowly. Harsh, fluorescent lights that gave him a headache almost instantly. The next thing he became aware of was the steady beeping sound he'd attributed to a parrot in his dream. Looking around, he found the source of the noise – a cardiac monitor beside his bed, dutifully recording each beat of his heart.

He was in a hospital room. Clean white walls and shiny linoleum floors. A narrow bed with scratchy sheets and a flat pillow. A range of machines and monitors displaying his vitals for the doctors and nurses who passed by. But by far the most interesting aspect of the room was the fact that he had company.

Seated in small cushioned chairs beside the room's windows were Matthew's parents. As he shifted and stirred, they took notice and quickly swept to his side. His mother's eyes filled with dewy tears.

"Matthew! We were so worried. How do you feel?"

Matthew rubbed his eyes, his vision still coming into focus in the bright lights.

"My head hurts," he mumbled. "But other than that I'm fine. What happened? Where am I?"

"We're at the Kennedy University Hospital. You fell in the backyard and hit your head on a rock. That's why your head hurts. You were unconscious for three days. The doctors weren't sure you were going to wake up at all." She sniffled, and wiped away a tear that had rolled down her cheek.

Matthew's head swam. He reached up and felt the cotton bandage wrapped tightly around his skull, identifying the sensitive spot near his left temple where he must have hit the rock. *Three days?* He thought, confused. *But I was in New York for three years. I lived there. I had a life there.* Clearing his throat, he struggled to voice his confusion without sounding like a crazy person.

"So... I've been here the whole time? All three days?"

"Yes, my son. Your father went out back to speak with you after your disagreement, and found you bleeding on the ground. We rushed you right over. You've been here since then."

Matthew looked up at his father, who still had not spoken. To his surprise, tears welled in Mark's eyes as well. He reached out and took his son's hand, clasping it tightly between his. Matthew swallowed hard to keep from crying himself, realizing in a flood of emotion just how much he'd missed his father. His voice broke as he spoke.

"I'm sorry, Dad."

Mark shook his head vigorously, the tears falling freely now.

"No, son. I'm sorry. Thank you for coming back to us."

Without another word, the family embraced one another in a tight hug. For the first time in a very long while, Matthew felt home.

Chapter 18

Matthew remained at the hospital for another two days after he woke up, while the doctors continued to examine the injury to his head and monitor for any signs of brain damage. All the while, his parents never left his side. They talked to him about the cases his father was working on, the unseasonably warm weather they'd been experiencing, the death of one of their old neighbors. It was the most Matthew could ever remember hearing them speak in such a short time.

Feeling uncharacteristically close to his long-estranged parents, Matthew opened up about details of his own life, as well. He told them about Jennifer at SB FINANCE, and his disappointing experience at the company Christmas party when he'd learned she was in a relationship. Growing up, he'd never talked to his parents about the girls he'd liked. Doing so now felt childish, yet strangely comforting.

He also shared his sense of being unfulfilled at his job as a consultant. He explained how he couldn't shake the feeling that there was something else he was supposed to be doing with his life, something more dynamic and creative. Such sentiments must have been uncomfortable for Mark Kim, ever the pragmatist, to hear, but to his credit he was patient and supportive of his son's confessions.

The one thing Matthew did not choose to divulge with his parents was his bizarre experience of living in New York City nearly a century earlier. That kind of story, he knew, was exactly the kind that landed you in a mental institution, no matter how understanding your parents behaved. Besides, as the hours passed in the hospital it seemed more and more likely that the whole thing had been some kind of crazy hallucination or dream he'd had while in a coma. That was certainly easier to explain than some sort of trauma-induced time travel.

By the time the Kim family was ready to leave the hospital, Matthew's head was healing quite nicely. The angry red gash on his temple had given way to a thin, shiny pink scar. The headache had diminished dramatically, but just in case, the doctors had written him a prescription for powerful painkillers.

Chapter 19

Seraphina Kim had insisted that Matthew stay at their home in New Jersey for a few days until he got his strength back. His father had already called the office in San Francisco to let them know what had happened, and Matthew's boss had told him to take all the time he needed. So Matthew returned home with his parents, reluctantly allowing them to dote on him for a couple days more. His mother made him tea while his father updated him on the lives of the other law associates at his firm, who had been family friends since Matthew's childhood.

It was wonderful to be at peace with his parents for the first time in years, but Matthew was eager to get back to San Francisco and get on with his life. There was change coming, he could feel it. He couldn't stand to sit idle any longer. He booked a flight back to the west coast, and set off to find his new calling. After running a few errands to pick up groceries and beer, he decided to spend his first day back soul-searching. He didn't call the office to tell them he was back in the city, so no one was expecting him anywhere. Instead, he sat at his desk in peace and tried to figure out where he was supposed to go next.

What are you looking for, Matthew? What exactly are you trying to find? Who do you want to be? He wracked his brain for answers but found none. There was nothing but the constant, nagging urge to *create*. For hours he searched job listings online, but nothing felt right. Around noon, he grew frustrated and shoved himself forcefully away from the desk and stomped to the kitchen to make lunch.

Standing before his open fridge, Matthew reached for items without thinking. He glided mindlessly around the kitchen, retrieving more items from the pantry and setting a pot of water on the stove to boil, not fully conscious of what he was making. About twenty minutes later, as he set a steaming bowl of pasta on his table, he broke from his reverie. The warm marinara sauce filled the air with the aromas of fresh vegetables, herbs, and expertly seasoned ground beef. Looking down at the dish he'd prepared, Matthew froze. Before his accident, he almost never cooked. When he did, it was minimalist and simple. He certainly never made sauces from scratch.

It didn't feel like a skill he'd developed on the spot. Cooking felt natural and practiced. *But that means...* People didn't just learn new skills while in a coma. A dream couldn't teach someone to julienne a carrot or poach an egg. Experiences did that. But for Matthew to have experienced such teachings… *It couldn't have just been a dream. It must have been… real?* Abandoning the pasta on the table, Matthew ran back to his desk and opened his laptop. He Googled the name Adelina Bianchi. There were thousands of hits for a woman by that name. An Italian fashion designer prominent in the early 20th century. Biani was real.

Chapter 20

Matthew's heart raced as he read an online biography of Adelina Bianchi. Everything he read matched up exactly with his memories of the enigmatic designer. He'd never heard of her before the accident, so he couldn't have made up the story in his head, right? Somehow, he must have met her. Somehow, he had actually been present in New York City between 1919 and 1922.

A picture of Biani on her biography page caught Matthew's eye. She was sitting on a couch, beaming up at someone off-camera. She wore a peculiar, angular black hat and a sharp fitted blazer over her black dress, her wrists and fingers adorned with chunky silver jewelry. Matthew couldn't help but smile at Biani's knowing grin, and her absolute comfort in her own unique style. She was inspirational.

Suddenly, it hit him. Inspirational. She was his inspiration. The person he was looking for, the person he wanted to emulate. Biani embodied rebellion and creativity and innovation. To find his own path, Matthew could follow hers. He too could design, and innovate, and create. He'd always been particularly interested in style and clothing, so why not give the fashion industry a try? He could design his own line, just like Biani had, and see where it took him.

Excitement over his hastily-made plan quickly gave way to stress and fear as Matthew realized he didn't know the first thing about designing a clothing line. He would need to educate himself on the basics of design, not to mention forming his own company from scratch. The obstacles seemed overwhelming. Then he heard Biani's words echoing in the back of his mind: *"Stay hungry, stay ambitious, and the sky's the limit."*

Taking a deep breath to gather his resolve, Matthew plunged forward into his future.

Chapter 21

The next day, Matthew returned to work at SB FINANCE. He had already made up his mind to pursue a new career path, but he knew it wasn't prudent to abandon a steady job before he had made any arrangements for future employment. His designer aspirations were still in the early development phase, and he needed a paycheck while he made plans for his dream job.

Everyone in the office seemed to have heard about his accident. His desk was littered with flowers and "Get Well Soon" cards, as though he would have magically benefitted from them on the other side of the country. Throughout the day, his coworkers made a point to stop by and see how he was doing. He was both surprised and touched by the outpouring of support.

Jason from Human Resources was one of the first to offer his sympathies. He clapped Matthew on the back and smiled warmly.

"How are ya feeling, buddy?"

"I'm fine, Jason. Just a bit of a lingering headache, that's all."

"Glad to hear it. You gave us all a good scare! Take a bit of a faceplant back in Jersey? Too much to drink, champ?"

"Yeah, I suppose so. I just sort of lost my balance. And then found the only rock in my parents' backyard with my head."

Jason chuckled, smacking Matthew on the back again.

"Perfect aim! Well, just wanted to let you know I talked to the higher-ups and they all understand your situation. You'll have a reduced caseload for as long as you need it, and you can come in late or leave early if you're not feeling too hot."

"Thanks Jason, I appreciate it. I really am doing a lot better though."

"Good good. Just let me know if there's anything else I can do for ya."

Matthew smiled politely as Jason walked away, then rubbed his aching head. He certainly was grateful for Jason's interest and support, but talking to the boisterous HR rep always left him craving the quiet solitude of a library.

Later, standing in the break room preparing his first cup of coffee of the day, Matthew was visited by a less grating well-wisher. Jennifer was just as beautiful as ever, wearing a long brown cardigan sweater over a snug white button-down and khaki slacks. Her green eyes sparkled as she smiled at him, perfect white teeth gleaming. Even as he felt his heart turn somersaults, Matthew thought to himself that some sort of green accent piece would really complete her outfit, and complement the emerald glow of her eyes. Now that he had acknowledged his creative side, he was seeing opportunities for its application everywhere.

"Hey, Matthew. How are you doing? We were all really worried when we heard about the accident."

"I'm doing a lot better, thanks. It's just a bump on the head; it's not as bad as everyone's making it out to be."

"Well that's a relief. You gave us all quite a scare! You were at your parents' house, right?"

"Yeah, my parents' place in New Jersey. Just tripped in the backyard. I guess it was actually pretty lucky, since if it had happened here it might have taken a while for someone to find me."

Jennifer's pretty face contorted into a frown of concern and sympathy.

"That could have been terrible! I'm really glad it all worked out okay. And please, if there's anything at all I can do to help make your life easier, don't hesitate to ask!"

"Thanks, Jennifer. Will do."

Jennifer's frown resolved once again into a winning smile, as she gave a small nod and turned and left the break room. Matthew returned to his coffee, adding a splash of creamer before heading back to his desk. He continued to receive a steady stream of visitors throughout the morning, as well as a few calls from relatives who had heard what happened from his parents. He did his best to be cheery and appreciative of all of the concern and support, but by midday his headache had worsened and he was growing tired of the pity. Finally he decided to take advantage of the offer to leave early as needed, and packed his things to head home.

Grabbing the stack of mail in his inbox, he quickly sorted through to dispose of any spam. The cover of this month's issue of *Technology Review* caught his eye, and he paused. The feature story was about 3D printing. Matthew had heard of the technology before, but didn't have a good understanding of how it worked or what the potential applications were. Folding the magazine under his arm, he left the office.

Chapter 22

Back at home, Matthew hummed to himself as he stirred a big pot of minestrone over the stove, breathing in the delightful smells of fresh vegetables, beans, and herbs. He ladled himself a bowl of the hot soup, removing the rest of the pot from heat. The leftovers would make for delicious meals later in the week. Setting the bowl on the table, he retrieved the *Technology Review* magazine from his briefcase and opened it to the story about 3D printing.

> *Already being hailed as "dream machines," 3D printers offer the exciting possibility of printing functional objects. Unlike traditional "subtractive" manufacturing methods, which can waste upwards of 95% of raw materials, 3D printing makes use of "additive" techniques. These additive machines use only the material necessary for the part being printed, so there is no waste. This technology also allows for an unprecedented freedom in terms of design possibilities, with far fewer constraints on potential geometries than traditional manufacturing techniques. Professor Richard Hague, of the Additive Manufacturing Research Group (AMRG) at Loughborough University, remarks about 3D printing that, "It changes the kind of products you can make and the way you design things. It's almost as close to Nirvana as you're ever going to get."*

The article went on to detail the different materials that had been used in 3D printing endeavors, including plastic thermopolymers and various metals. It also described the process of designing objects to be printed, by creating CAD files to model the desired object in 3 dimensions. The designer could then specify the orientation of the layers of material for the object, and the 3D printer would make their dream a reality. The technology was quickly gaining ground in the aerospace and biomedical industries, where there was a need for highly specialized parts and little room for waste or excess.

The most interesting part of the article to Matthew, however, was a tiny blurb near the end about other potential applications of 3D printing. The technology was making inroads in the fashion industry as a fun trend for creating articles such as sunglasses, shoes, or jewelry. The novelty items had gained some popularity, and there were even collaborations forming to attempt to 3D print garments like shirts or dresses. As he read, Matthew's eyes widened. *This is it,* he thought. *This is what I've been looking for. THIS is the future.*

Chapter 23

The next few weeks passed in a blur for Matthew, as November gave way to December and a cold chill settled in on the West Coast. Excited and intrigued by his discovery of the world of 3D printing, he found himself daydreaming elaborate futures for himself while at work, during his commute, as he ate dinner. He wanted to harness the power of the mysterious new technology and apply it to the fashion industry. If the futuristic printers worked the way he imagined they did, they would allow for brand-new, previously impossible designs, and unique new looks.

But where do I even begin? Matthew had to admit to himself that he didn't know anything about working in the world of fashion. Or 3D printing, for that matter. No designer in their right mind would hire a middle-aged consultant with zero industry experience whose only motivation for entering the field was a bizarre dream/coma/supernatural occurrence in which he'd met a quirky Italian woman named Adelina Bianchi. Not that he would even tell them that much. At best, he would be ridiculed for interpreting a dream as reality. At worst, he'd end up locked in a padded room for the foreseeable future.

His best option, it seemed, was to start fresh. He could start a company of his own. That way, he'd be free of any kind of pressure to conform to existing practices and ideologies. He could make his own business choices, his own design choices, his own marketing choices.

But Matthew had never started his own company. He had no experience managing a business, much less one in the fashion industry. Not to mention, his three-year (three-day?) jaunt in New York City had left him physically, mentally, and emotionally exhausted. If he was going to form his own start-up, he was going to need a partner.

Eager to move forward with his newly hatched idea, Matthew began to call on trusted friends to find his new business companion. First on the list was Jason Stark, his roommate at Dartmouth who now worked as an investment banker in Chicago.

"Jason Stark, how can I help you?"

"Jason! It's me, Matthew Kim."

"Matthew! It's so good to hear from you! Jesus, it's been years!"

"I know, I know! How have you been?"

"I've been good, man, I've been good! Sarah's pregnant again, so little Allie's going to have a baby brother soon."

"Well congratulations! That's amazing! Say hi to Sarah for me, too."

"I will, definitely. So how are you doing, dude?"

"I'm… well, I'm actually going through a bit of a transition period right now."

"Oh no, dude, were you laid off or something?"

"No, no, nothing like that… but I am actually looking to change career fields at the moment. But it's one-hundred-percent my decision."

"That so? You're in consulting now, right?"

"That's right. But I actually want to start my own company."

"Your own SB Finance?"

"A totally new direction, actually. Um… I want to start a fashion design company."

"Fashion? You mean like… clothes and shoes and stuff?"

"Exactly, yeah. Only we'll 3D print our clothes. It'll be the first line of exclusively 3D printed fashion items."

"Oh wow! That's… certainly different. How'd you decide to pursue that?"

"That's a long story. But the point of my calling is actually to ask if you might… Might be interested in joining me?"

"Joining you? I'm not sure I follow."

"I was wondering… I was wondering if you might want to be my partner. For my start-up. I realize it's a longshot and I know it's all out of the blue…"

"Oh, wow… I… I don't really know what to say. With the new baby coming and everything… I don't really think I'm in a position to start something new. I'm sorry, dude. It does sound like a neat idea though."

"No worries. I figured as much, just wanted to give it a shot. It sounds like you've got a great thing going there in Chicago, so I won't pester you about it! But do pass on my congratulations to the wife."

"Thanks, I will. Hey, let me know how everything goes. With the, uh… the shoes and the 3D printing and everything."

"Haha, thanks, I'll keep you posted. It was good talking to you, Jason."

"Yeah, it's always great catching up! Have a good one, dude."

Matthew sighed as he hung up the phone. He hadn't really been expecting anything different, but he'd had a glimmer of optimism that maybe Jason would be getting burned out in the fast-pace world of investment banking and might bring his keen business acumen to help his old roommate. Oh well.

Next on the list was Lisa Murray. They'd met at Oxford and dated briefly before an amicable split. They'd remained friends throughout Matthew's time abroad, and exchanged emails every now and then as they came across stories or articles about penguins. It was a running joke, since on their first date Matthew had asked Lisa what her favorite animal was. She had replied penguins, and, eager to form a connection, he had quickly replied "Me too!" Lisa saw right through the lie, and the two had shared many a laugh about penguins ever since.

Lisa picked up on the second ring.

"Matty! I haven't heard from you in months!" She was the only person in the world who called him Matty. He'd tried to insist that he preferred Matthew, but Lisa could be awfully persistent. He'd never actually admitted it, but he kind of liked the nickname when she used it.

"Hi Lisa! How are you?"

"I'm great! And yourself?"

"Good, good. I can't complain." Matthew elected not to tell Lisa about his recent medical issues. That would start a whole conversation that he really didn't want to get into.

"So, to what do I owe the pleasure, old friend?"

"It's a business proposition, actually."

"Oh really? Look, Matty, I told you you're too smart to sell yourself into male prostitution. Plus, I'm a married woman now."

The two laughed warmly, and Matthew fondly remembered back to their adventures at Oxford.

"Come on Lisa, you know I don't have the body for that line of work."

"Well maybe if you started running a few miles in the morning…"

"I hate running."

"Fair enough. I hate it too. Anyway, what's this proposition anyway?"

"I'm looking to start my own business."

"Ah, the big entrepreneur! What kind of business?"

"A fashion line, actually. I realize it's a little outside the lines for me, but I have this idea that 3D printing is the future of fashion, and I want to start getting involved in these new designs, and –"

"Whoa whoa whoa, slow down Matty!"

He took a deep breath to steady himself.

"Sorry. I'm just a little nervous about the whole deal."

"It's fine, it's fine. Just breathe. So where do I fit into this whole scheme?"

"Well... I'm actually looking for a business partner. Someone to help me start the company. I wanted to know if you'd be interested. Fifty-fifty ownership, profits, the whole deal."

There was a brief pause, a silence that grew tangibly more awkward to Matthew as the seconds ticked by. Finally, mercifully, Lisa spoke.

"I'm sorry, Matty. I just can't really afford to change career paths right now. I just got a promotion, and we're financially stable for the first time in years... I don't think I can ask my family to even take the chance of going back to the way it was."

"I understand."

"It really does sound like a neat idea though! And maybe once you get this thing off the ground and start making some money, I can contribute as an investor or something. But I just can't swing it right now."

"It's okay, Lisa, I understand. I knew it wasn't a realistic chance, but I just wanted to give it a shot. Thanks anyway!"

"Of course. And do keep in touch, man. I want to hear about the start-up and I don't want to go six months without hearing from you again!"

Matthew chuckled.

"Okay, yes ma'am. Take care, Lisa."

"You too. Bye bye."

There was a click on the line as Lisa hung up, and then an empty dial tone. Matthew knew he had no right to be disappointed. Still, he and Lisa would have made excellent business partners.

Skimming through his address book, Matthew made similar calls to six other good friends from school, hoping to find an interested partner. He continued to strike out, and he began to wonder if maybe this wasn't such a good idea after all.

Chapter 24

After an hour of frustrating phone calls, Matthew needed a break from sitting at his desk staring at his list of names and numbers. He decided to go for a drive, which often helped to clear his head. Grabbing his jacket, he headed out into the cold.

He drove on autopilot, paying little attention to the streets and neighborhoods he passed. His mind was elsewhere, wondering what Adelina might do in this situation. When he found himself in the parking lot of the San Francisco

International Airport, he had no memory of how he had gotten there.

Ordinarily, this would concern Matthew. He would think he was losing his mind, going into some weird early stage of dementia or something of that ilk. But in light of recent events, he had simply accepted that he might be crazy and he might not, but dwelling on the question would not accomplish anything. Instead, he blindly followed the invisible force that directed his actions.

He was pulled magnetically into the airport by said force, and he did not object. He approached the United ticket counter and purchased a one-way ticket to John Wayne Airport, in Orange County, California. Eerily, he could hear Adelina's voice in his head: *Return to your roots, Matthew. Find yourself.* He'd grown up in Orange County, often viewed as the land of the rich and superficial. After he'd left for Dartmouth, his parents had picked up and moved across the country to New Jersey, citing a need for a change in scenery. In reality, they'd just wanted to be a little closer to their only son.

Matthew passed quickly through security, having no bag to check or carry on. He found his gate and waited an hour until it was time to board. It occurred to him that he could have driven to Orange County in less time than it would take to fly there, but he simply accepted that this was the magnetic force's plan. The flight was about forty-five minutes, and he slept from takeoff to touchdown, completely at ease. He then hailed a cab to his childhood home.

Arriving in front of the house he'd grown up in, Matthew paid the cabbie and stepped out onto the curb. He remained there long after the taxi drove away, just staring at the house. He wasn't sure how long he stood like that, in the chilly December afternoon air, when the sound of a heavy door closing nearby broke his focus.

Turning, Matthew saw a large, burly, redheaded man exiting the house next door. He recognized him instantly. His childhood neighbor and best friend.

"John Wright? Is that you?"

The redheaded man looked up, shocked silent for a moment, then broke into a big toothy grin.

"Matthew Kim! Holy hell, it's been years!"

John crossed the yard quickly to embrace Matthew in a bear hug. As always, Matthew was a bit concerned that his ribcage would be crushed in the ex-linebacker's grip. His pained grimace gave way to a smile as John released him, clapping him on the back with one of his gigantic hands.

"What brings you back to the old stomping grounds, man?" John's booming voice was warm and welcoming.

"Just stopped by for a visit, really. No particular reason. How about you?"

"Visiting the old lady. Dad died of a stroke a few years ago, so I like to check in on her every few weeks and see how she's doing."

"Oh my…, I'm sorry John. I didn't even know. How is your mother?"

"She's doing just fine, thanks. She decided to take up tennis and I think she's in better shape than me these days!"

John's massive muscular shoulders bounced up and down as he laughed.

"Well that's good to hear. Do you still live in the area?"

"Nah, but I'm not too far. I'm working on my PhD at CalTech, so I live up in Pasadena. Pretty easy drive to come back and visit."

"CalTech! Wow! That's incredible. I take it you're still into all of that programming stuff?"

In high school, John had been notorious for his computer skills. He was a bit of a contradiction as both a jock and a geek, but no one ever dared to make fun of the gigantic genius football player.

"Yup, computer science. It's good stuff. What have you been up to?"

Matthew hesitated for a moment.

"I… well, mostly just working, I guess. I'm at SB FINANCE over in San Francisco, and it's usually pretty hectic. I'm actually considering a bit of a career change. I also just got back from a visit to my parents, too."

"Where do they live now? I know they moved out when you went to Dartmouth, but I couldn't remember where."

"New Jersey."

"Gotcha. And how are they doing?"

"They're well. Enjoying the cooler weather, I think."

"Can't blame 'em! This summer was sweltering. Although I wouldn't mind a bit more sunshine right now. So what's this career change business?"

"I think I want to start my own company."

"Wow, look at this guy! Mister entrepreneur! Your own advisory firm?"

"A fashion line, actually. Which I realize sounds totally crazy, but I think it could be a good fit for me. I've always wanted to do something more creative."

"Huh! Well it's a bit unexpected, sure, but not crazy. Man, I remember back in high school you were always writing stories and everything. I could definitely see you getting into the artistic stuff."

It was the most accepting and nonchalant response Matthew had received thus far to his harebrained scheme to be a designer. He felt a rush of affection towards his old friend.

"Hey, what are you up to tonight? Do you want to grab dinner or something before I head back to San Francisco?"

"I was actually planning on heading back up to Pasadena. There's a party tonight that I wanted to check out. You should come with me! When's your flight?"

Since he hadn't actually booked a return flight yet, Matthew wasn't sure how to answer. He was eager to get back home and continue his hunt for a partner, but he was also emotionally drained. A fun night out with an old friend could be exactly the release he needed. Besides, he was trying to be more spontaneous.

"Not 'till tomorrow. I'd love to check out one of your nerdy CalTech parties!"

John beamed.

"Ha, I just hope you can keep up! You know the saying with us engineers: work hard, play hard."

"Bring it on!"

Chapter 25

A short while later, Matthew found himself sitting in the passenger seat of John's black Kia coupe, listening the classic rock that was blasting over the radio. He felt completely relaxed for the first time in recent memory. This was nice. He felt that somehow, some way, this was what he was meant to be doing.

The drive to Pasadena took about 45 minutes. When they arrived, John gave Matthew a brief tour of his tiny apartment and introduced him to his roommate, Marcus. Marcus was about 5'8", black, and wore thick glasses. He was in his mid-20's, a graduate student in chemical engineering. He smiled and politely shook Matthew's hand without saying a word.

John clicked on the TV and selected a football game. Pittsburgh Steelers vs. Chicago Bears. Matthew didn't follow the NFL, and had little interest in either team, but he was happy to watch mindlessly and listen to John's running commentary ("Oh come on, that was holding!" "If he'd seen the option there and they'd be in the endzone by now.") Marcus began preparing burgers on a portable George Forman grill, chuckling occasionally at his roommate's outbursts.

The burgers were done by halftime, and the three men loaded them up with cheese, ketchup, and lettuce and ate them along with a bag of potato chips while sitting on the couch. Matthew was suddenly ravenous, realizing he hadn't eaten anything all day, with the exception of a small packet of pretzels on the plane. He bit into the cheeseburger with gusto, and was surprised by the complex flavor of the beef.

"Paprika, cayenne pepper, and ground mustard?" Matthew asked abruptly.

John squinted at Matthew, confused, but Marcus broke into a wide grin.

"That's right. My dad's favorite recipe. How do you like it?"

"It's delicious!"

Marcus nodded proudly, and John shook his head in bewilderment.

"You foodies, man… I don't get how you guys do it. It just tastes like a burger to me."

Matthew looked at Marcus and shrugged.

"I don't know… it takes a little practice I guess. But there's definitely something to be said for genetics, too, I bet."

"Well I guess I missed out on that gene. For me, meat is meat is meat."

They all chuckled, and resumed watching the game. Their seasoning conversation had broken the ice between Matthew and Marcus, and the three chatted amicably for the next hour. The game ended, with the Bears victorious, around 11 o' clock. John hopped to his feet.

"Party time!"

Matthew tried and failed to stifle a yawn. John laughed.

"I saw that! No getting tired now. Time to rally, my friend."

Matthew smiled and nodded, shaking out his limbs to wake himself up. Ten minutes later, the three men were out the door and on their way.

Chapter 26

Marcus drove. Matthew sat in the backseat of the cobalt grey Camry and tried to shake off his nerves. He'd always suffered from a touch of social anxiety, and couldn't wait to get a drink to settle himself down. *What are you worried about, anyway?* John had promised there would be no shortage of geeky engineers at the party, so even at his worst Matthew would not stick out for poor social skills. That said,

John had then added, there would also be more than a few lovely ladies, so Matthew had better bring his A-game.

Their destination was only about a ten minute drive away. As they parked the car and walked toward the door to the apartment, Matthew could tell that the party was already in full swing. Music was blasting through the open windows, and the voices of happily drunk graduate students could be heard through breaks in the songs.

A petite Asian woman greeted them at the door. She had perfectly styled long black hair with golden streaks throughout, and wore black leggings beneath an oversized denim Oxford button-down with the sleeves rolled up. An eye-catching emerald necklace hung around her neck, the gemstone catching the light every so often. She quickly embraced John and Marcus each in a friendly hug.

"Oh good! Glad you guys could make it!"

"Of course, Jess, thanks for the invite!"

"And who's your friend here?"

John stepped back and patted Matthew on the back.

"This here is Matthew. He was my neighbor growing up, if you can believe that! We were best friends all throughout high school. We happened to run into each other this afternoon so I invited him along. I hope that's okay."

Jess smiled, and her white teeth were perfectly straight.

"Of course! The more the merrier! My name's Jessica. But everyone calls me Jess," she said, extending a hand towards Matthew. "I'm in the computer science department with John."

"Nice to meet you, Jess." Matthew shook her outstretched hand and tried to keep his voice even and calm.

After the introductions, Jess led them into the crowded, noisy apartment. She had to shout to be heard over the music and conversations.

"So there's drinks in the kitchen – Steph just brought back more ice and cups so we should be fine there. There's also snacks in the living room, and the bathroom's down the hall on your left. Have a great time, guys!"

With that, Jess disappeared back into the crowds to resume her post greeting newcomers at the door. Marcus quickly drifted away too, chatting up a pretty young blonde standing by the speakers.

John tapped Matthew's shoulder and gestured for him to follow him over to the kitchen to get a drink. There were all manner of alcoholic beverages displayed on the kitchen counter – for broke graduate students, they definitely managed to splurge on booze. John poured himself a bourbon with 7-Up in a red plastic Solo cup. Matthew stuck with a beer, knowing he should be very careful to pace himself.

With drinks in hand, they made their way into the living room, where they joined a small circle of three men and one woman who were talking enthusiastically about something. All four smiled when they saw John, greeting him with high-fives and fist bumps. John quickly introduced his old friend to his new ones.

"Guys, this is my friend Matthew. He and I go way, way back. Matthew, this is Jason Peck" – he gestured to a short, prematurely balding white man with thick glasses - "Akhil Gupta" – a tall, thin Indian man with a mischievous grin – "Alex Lee" – an Asian man just a few inches taller than Matthew, dressed in jeans and a hoodie – "and Scarlet Love" – the only woman in the group, a short, ponytailed brunette with an athletic build and piercing green eyes. "These guys are also grad students at CalTech. Jason's in computer science with me and Alex is in astrophysics. Akhil and Scarlet are in the materials science department. "

Matthew's head spun with the new information, and he concentrated hard on committing the names and faces to memory so that he didn't embarrass himself later. He took a sip from his beer, and noticed Scarlet's green eyes were locked on him.

"So what brings you to Pasadena, Matthew?"

He gulped quickly, hoping he didn't seem too eager or frantic.

"I grew up in Orange County with John. I was back in town visiting and ran into him, and he invited me up here."

She nodded, satisfied for the time being, and the group resumed its previous conversation. Akhil elbowed John, smirking.

"We were just hearing all about Scarlet's weekend with Louis."

"The accountant guy?"

"Yup! Apparently there was a bit of trouble in paradise."

"I'm not surprised, the guy was a dweeb."

"The dweebiest!"

Scarlet smacked Akhil on the shoulder.

"Alright, alright already. Enough ragging on Louis. He was a nice guy, we just weren't a great fit."

"Because you actually have a personality?"

"He had a personality! It was just… we just… ugh. Fine. He was a dweeb." She gave a defeated sigh and the guys all laughed.

John patted her gently on the back.

"Don't worry, Scar. You'll find someone who can actually carry on a conversation someday."

Scarlet rolled her eyes and grinned.

"Okay, I think that's more than enough time spent discussing my failed love life. I'm ready for another beer. Who's with me?"

Chapter 27

After the first drink, Matthew loosened up considerably, and the night seemed to fly by. The CalTech friends were warm and welcoming, and in no time he was included in their enthusiastic, buzzed conversations. He and Alex exchanged humorous stories about some of the more extreme lengths their parents had taken to ensure that they were adequately preparing themselves for college applications – starting in about the second grade. Scarlet gave a heartfelt rant on her dislike of being stereotyped as a nerd simply by virtue of the school she had attended, and Jason surprised and impressed them all by knowing every line of a rap by EMINA, a new emerging hip-hop group, that blasted over the speakers.

As the conversation turned toward potential employment opportunities for John and Jason after they finished up their PhD's, Matthew remembered his purpose in visiting California. He was here to find answers, to make progress towards finding his purpose. He'd been drawn to the airport that morning for a reason, right? What if that reason was to find the business partner he'd been searching for?

As soon as the thought crossed his mind, Matthew became antsy and excited. What if his future partner was right here in this room? What if he or she was right in front of him? His eyes landed on Scarlet, perched on the arm of a sofa in front of him, and he could not draw them away. It was her. He was suddenly sure of it. She was the partner he'd been looking for.

Matthew waited for a short lull in the conversation, then tapped on John's shoulder.

"Hey man, could I talk to you in private for a minute?"

John stood without asking any questions, and the rest of the group paid them little mind. Matthew led John to the far corner of the room.

"It's her!" Matthew blurted as soon as they were out of earshot of the others.

"Come again?"

"Scarlet. It's her."

"What's her?"

"I think she could be my new business partner."

"Umm… okay? Did you talk to her about this?"

"Not yet."

"So you think this why, exactly?"

"I just have this gut feeling, I guess."

"Care to elaborate on that?"

"It's hard to explain. I just feel like we're connected somehow."

"Seriously, dude, I'm gonna need a little more of an explanation."

"Fine. For example, she hates being stereotyped as a nerd, right?"

"Uh huh…"

"And I totally relate to that. I hate being stereotyped as some boring, straight-laced numbers guy."

"How profound."

"There's more, okay? Remember what my favorite book was when we were growing up?"

John squinted his face up, trying to remember back to their high school days.

"*The Scarlet Letter*, I think?"

"Exactly!"

Matthew smiled up at John expectantly, as if this explained everything. John was not impressed.

"So because her name happens to be in the title of a book you once liked, that means you should start a business together?"

"All I'm saying is that it's a sign! I don't think it's a coincidence. I just have this feeling that she's the person I've been looking for."

"Well, you might want to talk to her about all this before you go signing her name on any business loans."

"I know, I know. Do you think you could maybe vouch for me? Just let her know I'm not a lunatic or anything?"

"I'm not particularly convinced of that fact myself, at the moment. But if it means this much to you, sure. I'll do it."

"Thanks, John. I really appreciate it."

"Just wait here a minute."

John left Matthew standing in the corner, and returned to where the others were still sitting and chatting. He leaned in and spoke into Scarlet's ear, his words inaudible from the other side of the room. In response to whatever he said, Scarlet's emerald green eyes snapped over to Matthew. She seemed to size him up for a moment, then stood and followed John back to the corner. She stood directly in front of Matthew, her hands on her hips.

"So John tells me you have some sort of proposition for me? I should warn you, I'm not at all interested in dating at the moment."

"No, it's nothing like that! It's more of a business proposition."

"Oh?"

"I'm looking for a business partner. I want to start my own company."

"I'm a grad student. I'm working on my PhD, remember? What kind of start-up is it, anyway?"

The pounding music was starting to give Matthew a headache, and he didn't want to botch this opportunity with Scarlet.

"Do you think we could meet for coffee sometime and talk about it? I don't think this is the best environment for this discussion."

Scarlet raised one eyebrow, clearly skeptical. Matthew looked pleadingly at John, who sighed and turned to Scarlet.

"Scar, I know this guy sounds crazy. And if it was anyone else, I'd blow him off. But Matthew's one of my oldest and most trusted friends, and I think you should give him a chance to explain his ideas. One coffee. That's all he's asking."

For one long minute, the young materials scientist considered the inexplicably eager stranger standing before her. Finally, she shook her head and shrugged.

"Fine, what the hell. One coffee. I've got some free time tomorrow morning. How about 11 o'clock at the

Starbucks on Fair Oaks Avenue? John can give you directions."

"Perfect! That would be great. Thank you so much!"

Matthew could barely contain his smile.

Chapter 28

It was after 2:00 A.M. when Matthew, John, and Marcus finally arrived back at the apartment. John drove, as Marcus had had a few too many drinks. As soon as they got back, Marcus disappeared into his room to pass out. John found a pillow and a spare blanket and tossed both onto the sofa for Matthew, who wasted no time brushing away the potato chip crumbs and making himself a nest. All three men were sound asleep before 2:30.

The tropical breeze tousled his hair as he stretched out in the early afternoon sun. Matthew slowly got to his feet. He wiggled his toes in the sand for a moment before strolling over to a lone palm tree, which offered a small pocket of shade. The soft sand was cooler here, and he lingered, just watching the cerulean waves lapping rhythmically at the shore. A woman's voice broke his trance.

"Whatcha looking at?"

Matthew turned and saw Scarlet Love standing just a few feet to his right. Her petite frame was tan and lean, and the sun overhead brought out reddish undertones in her rich brown hair. She was wearing only a skimpy blue bikini that complemented her eyes brilliantly. There was a small silver piercing in her navel, and Matthew had to stop himself from staring. She laughed and shook her head, causing her wavy brown tresses to cascade around her shoulders.

"Here, take this."

She extended to Matthew a delicate martini glass filled with some sort of orange-ish pink frozen drink. It tasted of sweet tropical fruit, with a subtle alcoholic bite. He smiled at Scarlet, who was now looking up at him expectantly.

"Ready to get to work?"

Matthew awoke to the morning sun pouring in through the living room window. He glanced at the clock on the cable box below the television. 9:14 A.M. He sat up and stretched his arms above his head, yawning. He heard the soft clink of glass behind him, and turned to find Marcus standing in the kitchen with his back to him, making a pot of coffee. Marcus heard Matthew yawn, and spun around.

"I'm sorry, did I wake you?"

"No, you're fine! I didn't even hear you come in."

"Oh, good. Want some coffee? It's nice and strong."

"That would be great, thanks!"

Matthew got to his feet, shuffling to the bathroom to pee and wash his face. By the time he returned to the living room, there was a cup of fresh black coffee steaming on the coffee table, waiting for him. Marcus carried over a bowl of

152

sugar and a half-empty gallon of milk, sitting beside Matthew on the couch and preparing his own cup of coffee with just a small splash of milk. Stealing glances out of the corner of his eye, Matthew took notice of Marcus' physical appearance. He looked like hell. His eyes were puffy and bloodshot, and he moved gingerly, as if in pain. It was also clear that he was fighting back waves of nausea. The poor guy was very obviously in the throes of a killer hangover.

Matthew said nothing, trying to move quietly to avoid contributing to a possible headache in his kind host. He cringed when the spoon he used to stir the sugar in his coffee accidentally clinked against the cup, but Marcus didn't seem to notice. He was reclined against the back of the couch, sipping coffee and staring off into space. The silence was not uncomfortable, but Matthew was still relieved when John came stumbling into the kitchen, yawning loudly and rubbing his eyes. He smiled when he saw his roommate and friend.

"How's it going, party animals?" He paused for just a moment as he squinted at them, then laughed. "Oh my, Marcus, you look like you got hit by a truck or something."

"Kinda feels like it, too."

"Need some Advil?"

"Already took four."

"Lots of fluids, then. Get hydrated."

"I know."

With a long sigh, Marcus pushed off the couch and shuffled to the bathroom. John chuckled again, then gave Matthew a playful punch in the arm.

"Want some breakfast?"

"Please."

John walked into the kitchen and opened the fridge. He seemed disappointed with the selection. He then searched the cabinets over the stove, and found a box of Frosted Flakes. He set the cereal on the counter triumphantly, grinning over at Matthew.

Matthew couldn't help but smile back. Growing up, the two boys used to have breakfast together some mornings when Matthew's parents went to work early. This tended to be cereal, since they were often in a hurry to catch the bus, and Frosted Flakes had been a mutual favorite.

John set out two bowls and two spoons on the counter, and retrieved the milk from where it had been left on the coffee table. Both men prepared their cereal in silence, then sunk into the leather couch once more. John flicked on the television, selecting an old Arnold Schwarzenegger movie.

After finishing up his Flakes, Matthew asked to use John's bathroom to take a quick shower. It was bad enough that he would be meeting Scarlet in the same clothes as the night before. The least he could do was make sure he didn't smell. John drew him a quick map of the streets of Pasadena, marking the Starbucks on Fair Oaks Avenue with a large star. He'd offered to give Matthew a ride there, but it was a nice sunny day and Matthew hoped that the chilly fresh air would help him wake up a bit.

He left the apartment just after 10:30, and arrived at the Starbucks about five minutes before 11:00. The small shop was abuzz with the quiet bustle of young professionals and students seeking caffeine to fend off the late morning slump, but Matthew had no trouble finding a pair of soft maroon armchairs in one corner, separated by a small circular glass table. He set his jacket in one and sat in the other.

He didn't have to wait long. Scarlet entered the coffee shop at precisely 11:00. She wore a long black coat over a tan sweater and dark wash blue jeans, which disappeared into sleek black leather boots. She scanned the café for a moment before her intense green eyes locked onto Matthew, and she made her way through the crowds to where he was sitting. He stood as she reached him, shaking her hand and thanking her for agreeing to meet with him. She simply nodded and set her own jacket on the seat he had just vacated. Wordlessly, the pair drifted across the shop to the end of the line.

As they waited for the line to inch forward, Matthew shifted his weight uncomfortably from one foot to the other. He wasn't sure what to make of Scarlet's reticence. She didn't seem angry, per se, but she also didn't exactly seem excited about their meeting. He decided not to pester her with small talk in line.

After minutes that felt like hours to Matthew, they reached the front of the line. He ordered a cappuccino, which he'd become quite fond of while in Europe for grad school, and she ordered a latte. She reached for her wallet, but he quickly waved her off.

"No, no, it's on me! This was my idea!" She gave him a sideways look, still sizing him up, but put away her money and let him pay. An overly peppy young barista promptly handed them their coffees with a smile and a jaunty tilt of her blonde pony-tailed head.

They returned to the maroon armchairs and took their respective seats, and finally Scarlet spoke.

"So, what's this all about?"

Matthew was relieved that the young woman had finally broken her silence. He took a quick sip from his cup, burning his tongue on the hot coffee.

"I'm looking for a business partner."

"What kind of business?"

"Fashion design. I want to start a company."

Scarlet raised her eyebrows skeptically, scanning Matthew's wrinkled day-old clothes. He didn't exactly look the part.

"Are you in the fashion industry currently?"

"No, I'm in consulting."

"So this is… what, some kind of midlife crisis?"

"I prefer to think of it as an inspired career shift."

"Inspired by what, exactly?"

"An experience I had recently."

"Oh? Did you dabble as a supermodel?"

Matthew ignored the sarcastic edge to her voice.

"I met a designer. She helped open my eyes to new opportunities."

"So why not work with her?"

"She's… not really available."

"Too important to take on a nobody, huh?"

"She's dead, actually."

Scarlet's eyes widened in shock.

"Shoot, I'm sorry. I didn't mean to… I didn't realize…"

"It's fine, it's fine. No offense taken. It's not a sensitive issue. She died years ago."

"Does that mean you've been looking for a partner for years?"

"Not exactly. I actually saw her just last month."

Now Scarlet frowned, staring hard into Matthew's eyes in an attempt to discern whether he was joking, crazy, or something else entirely. When he did not laugh or wink, she leaned away slightly in her chair.

"So you're some kind of medium? You talk to ghosts and all that? I should warn you, I don't believe in any of that superstitious bullshit."

"Not a ghost. I saw her. In the flesh. Her name was Adelina Bianchi and she lived in New York during the early 1920's. That's when I met her."

Scarlet rolled her eyes.

"You look pretty good for someone who's well over 100 years old."

"Well I was this age when I met her. It was just last month. I had… an unusual experience."

"Yeah? Was it hard drugs?"

"I'm not actually sure what it was. I know this is going to sound completely ludicrous, but somehow I went back in time. I fell and hit my head, and when I woke up I was in New York City in 1919. I spent three years there, and then one day I fell again and woke up back in the present day."

"Sounds like a hallucination to me."

"Maybe. But all I know is I was conscious of every day of those three years. And the woman I met, Biani… she was real. You can Google her. And everything she told me is consistent with her biographies. It sounds crazy. I realize that. But that's what happened."

Scarlet leaned back even further into her chair and closed her eyes, processing the unlikely story she'd just been told. Matthew sipped nervously at his coffee, desperately hoping she wouldn't stand up and walk out on him. After a long moment, Scarlet shook her head, and reached for her coat. Matthew made one last effort.

"Wait! Let me try and prove it to you!"

Scarlet glared at him, clearly fed up with the conversation.

"And how exactly would you do that?"

"You can ask me questions about my time in New York. I'll answer them based on my experiences, and you can look online to confirm or deny what I'm saying."

The pretty young grad student shifted her weight forward again, resting her chin in her hands, her elbows on the circular table between them. She was studying Matthew's face for sincerity once more, and after searching his eyes, she sighed.

"Fine. One last chance. One wrong answer and I'm out of here, and you agree never to contact me again, understood?"

Matthew nodded so enthusiastically he hurt his neck.

"All right then. Let's get started."

Chapter 29

Matthew slumped back in his seat, catching his breath. It was nearly 2 o' clock in the afternoon, and he had just spent hours fielding every possible question Scarlet could think of to try and trip him up. She was still holding her phone in front of her, an incredulous look plastered across her face as she scanned pored over countless websites and documents. They had finished their coffee ages ago, and had been present for the ebb and flow of customers before, during, and after the lunch rush. Not that they'd noticed. Neither had moved from their chair.

Scarlet slowly lowered her phone to the table. For once she wasn't looking at Matthew. Instead, she was staring off into space, her gaze unfocused as she processed the situation.

"So either you have worked out some extremely clever ruse, or somehow this ridiculous story actually happened... And I haven't decided what I believe just yet. But ignoring all that, you've decided, for one reason or another, to start a fashion company, correct?"

"That's right."

"And you want me to help you."

"To be my partner, yes."

"Do you also realize I have no more experience in this industry than you?"

"I do."

"So why the heck would you want me for a partner?"

The question was a bit harder to answer than the ones about his employment and experiences in New York City. He didn't have a good response thought out for this one. He gave a hopeless shrug.

"I really don't know. I just have a feeling, I guess. I've been searching for a partner for weeks and when I met you, something clicked. I don't suppose you believe in fate?"

"None of that superstitious bullshit, remember?"

"Fine. Well I guess all I can say is that I believe our paths crossed for a reason. And I know it sounds insane but somehow I think that we would make great business partners."

"Great partners running a business we know nothing about. Do you even have any ideas for designs?"

"I've started a few sketches, actually. Still very rough, but they're ideas at least."

"What makes you think a couple of rookies like us would even be able to gain traction in the fashion world?"

"Because our designs won't be like everybody else's. We'd be pioneers of new materials."

"Such as?"

"I think we could create lines of entirely 3D-printed materials."

Scarlet's eyes widened.

"Did John tell you about my research?"

"I'm sorry?"

"Did he tell you I work in a lab that specializes in 3D-printing?"

Matthew shook his head no, a smile slowly spreading across his face. The shock began to fade from Scarlet's, and she grinned too.

"Maybe there's something to this fate thing, after all… Look, I'm starving and I'm way behind on homework. Give me some time to process all this. Do you have a card with your number?"

Matthew did, and slid it across the table. She picked it up, placed it in the back pocket of her blue jeans, grabbed her jacket and left the café, never looking back.

Chapter 30

Shortly after Scarlet's departure, Matthew stepped outside into the bracing cool air, and hailed a cab to the airport. He purchased a ticket on the next flight to San Francisco, which departed in two hours. He made his way through security, purchased a sandwich at a small kiosk, and took a seat at his gate. Feeling enthused by the turn the conversation with Scarlet had taken, he found a pen on a corner table and began to sketch out new designs on the napkin that had come with his sandwich. Long, bold lines. Sharp accents. Clothing that would make a statement.

He soon ran out of space on the napkin. He set the pen down where he had found it, and folded the napkin and placed it in his shirt pocket. Before too long, it was time to board. Matthew found his seat quickly and settled in. He was too excited and caffeinated to sleep, and spent the short flight staring out the window and daydreaming of the future.

His car was waiting for him at the airport. By the time he got home, it was nearly 6 o'clock. He set to work preparing a deliciously savory chicken marsala, humming quietly to no tune in particular. The sauce was starting to give off a truly mouth-watering aroma when the sound of the phone ringing broke his reverie. Matthew fished his cell phone out of his pocket. Not a number he recognized. He held the phone between his ear and his chin as he continued to work on his dinner.

"Hello?"

"Matthew?"

"Scarlet? Is that you?"

"Yeah. Hey, is this a bad time?"

"No, not at all! Just making dinner but I can put you on speaker!"

He nearly dropped his phone into the pot of pasta while he fumbled for the speaker button.

"Okay, all set. So what's up?"

Scarlet sighed at the other end of the line.

"Well, I know I told you I was going to think about this whole partnership thing. But I realized I'm a terrible decision-maker. So if I'm going to do this, I have to just take the plunge and commit to it now, while I'm still feeling stupidly optimistic about the whole thing."

Matthew said nothing, scared to jinx it.

"This is probably a huge mistake. In fact, almost definitely. I don't even know you. I don't know anything about fashion. But what the hell. I'm young. I have to take these risks now or I never will."

Matthew had stopped breathing.

"So I guess what I'm saying is yes. I'm in. I'll be your business partner for this ridiculous fashion start-up."

He let out the breath he'd been holding in one relieved *whoosh.*

"Oh Scarlet, I'm so glad to hear it! This is excellent news. I really do have a good feeling about this. I think we could pull this off."

"All right, all right, calm down. We need to get practical about this. Do you have a business plan?"

"Oh… no, not yet."

"Well that's our first step then. Are you free tomorrow to discuss plans?"

"Sure! I'll work from home tomorrow. I'll be available all day."

"Great. I'll call in the morning then. We'll get this thing rolling. Talk to you later, Matthew."

"Bye Scarlet!"

There was a soft beep as the line was disconnected, and Matthew stared at his phone in shock. He couldn't believe it. The harebrained plan was one step closer to becoming a reality. She'd said yes!

He couldn't stop smiling, not then and not as he ate his dinner. Not when he did the dishes and not when he watched

"Criminal Minds" on TV afterwards. He kept right on smiling as he changed into pajamas, brushed his teeth, and got into bed. He smiled himself to sleep.

Chapter 31

Matthew's phone rang at precisely 9:00 AM, and he knew without looking that it would be Scarlet. He'd been up since 7, drinking coffee and fidgeting while he watched the news and waited for her call.

"Good morning, Scarlet!"

"Good morning yourself. Ready to talk shop?"

"Yes ma'am!"

"Good. I should warn you I don't really know where to begin. I've never started a company before."

"That makes two of us."

"But I figured getting our vision straight would be a good place to begin. Let's hammer out some of the details of exactly what it is we're going for here."

"Great, I agree. So the basic idea is to start a small fashion boutique. With designs inspired by the work of Adelina Bianchi, and possibly some influence from organic food images. Making use of 3D printing technology to create unprecedented new designs and structures... How's that?"

"It's a start. I think we should also focus on making our materials and production process very environmentally friendly. If we're going to do this whole thing with the 3D printing, we should also be forward-thinking in regards to our waste and carbon footprint."

"That's an excellent idea. We could brand ourselves as this very futuristic and trend-setting company, using cutting-edge technology and preserving a better world for posterity."

"Right. I don't know of any other fashion lines out there right now doing anything like this. I think with my background in materials science we'll have an advantage over any possible competition."

"I agree. So I guess our target demographic would be upper-middle class, at least until we can find a way to drive costs down without compromising our principles. We'll design for both men and women. Most likely the younger crowd, who tend to be more open to new technologies and more passionate about saving the planet."

"That all makes sense to me. I think our biggest issue is going to be funding. This 3D printing technology is not cheap. At all. And of course we'll need to find a space to operate out of. How are we going to finance it all?"

"I was thinking of creating a Kickstarter account, at least to begin with. We can both work our connections through friends, family, coworkers, to find anyone who might be looking to invest. I have a chunk of money in savings that I can contribute, as well."

"Okay. While you get the Kickstarter up and running, I'll look into pricing for a 3D printer, as well as what it might cost to rent out one at a university or private facility, at least for the first few prototypes. I'll also do some research on environmentally friendly textiles."

"Perfect. I'll start putting out feelers to find some potential investors, and continue working on design sketches."

"Sounds like a plan. Check back in tomorrow with progress?"

"Works for me. Talk to you tomorrow, Scarlet."

"Bye, partner."

Matthew hung up the phone and hopped up from his armchair, nearly spilling his coffee. He dashed to his desk and began to work on the Kickstarter account. He discovered that nearly 2,000 fashion projects had already been successfully funded with the site's help, a total of over 40 million dollars. He couldn't help but feel a flurry of hope at seeing the numbers.

His hope began to falter, though, as he discovered the statistics for project success. Only 18% of projects seeking less than 50,000 dollars reached their funding goals, and only

7% of projects seeking 100,000 dollars or more. Matthew decided their best shot would be to start with a (relatively) smaller fundraising goal, and plan on using a university 3D printer or purchasing a small-scale one to use to furnish their product prototypes. Hopefully, these prototypes would inspire enough interest that larger donations would come in to fuel full-scale production.

He set the target funding to 50,000 dollars, with a time limit of six months. The timing would be tight, but neither he nor Scarlet could afford to commit to the project much longer than that without any kind of paycheck. If they hadn't reached their goal in six months, they would set down their sketchbooks and return to the real world.

For a project description, he did his best to summarize what he and Scarlet had discussed that morning; a forward-thinking fashion startup based on the principles of sustainable, environmentally-friendly production and a fresh take on the vintage styles of Adelina Bianchi, making use of cutting-edge 3D-printing technology to manufacture materials.

Matthew had just hit the "Complete" button to finalize the Kickstarter project when his cell phone rang for the second time that morning. It was his mother.

GEN SAN FRANCISCO Part II Coming Soon

"UNCOMMON PARTNERSHIP"

ABOUT THE AUTHORS

Occy Yang is a businessman and attorney in Seattle, Washington. When not practicing business or real estate law, Occy spends his time on producing novels and designing card games. Occy always wanted to write an entertaining story that celebrates America's entrepreneurial generation. He also believes such entrepreneurship increases social mobility and diversity in this great nation. Occy holds a BA from Dartmouth College, an MBA from INSEAD in France, a JD from Cornell Law School, and an MPP from Harvard University. For coming years, Occy aspires to promote and connect people and emerging companies from his favorite cities: Palo Alto, Seattle, San Francisco, Irvine, Singapore, and Seoul.

Katie Gorick was born and raised in northern Virginia. She received a degree in Biological Engineering from the Massachusetts Institute of Technology, where she graduated with a prefect GPA (5.0 on a 5.0 scale). At MIT, Katie was a member of the Tau Beta Pi engineering honor society and a four-year varsity rower for the lightweight women's crew team. Since then, she has decided to return to her home state and pursue a PhD in Biomedical Engineering at the University of Virginia. She loves sports and outdoor activities, live music and dancing, and good food. She hopes to someday have a career designing targeted medications to more effectively treat diseases and reduce harmful side effects.

Contact Information:

Please, feel free to contact me at oscar.yang@siliconberry.com. We appreciate all kind emails.

Occy Yang